RENDEZVOUS IN VERACRUZ

RENDEZVOUS IN VERACRUZ

by Carolyn G. Hart

PUBLISHED BY
M. EVANS AND COMPANY, INC., NEW YORK
AND DISTRIBUTED IN ASSOCIATION WITH
J. B. LIPPINCOTT COMPANY
PHILADELPHIA AND NEW YORK

To my aunt, Vivian Akin Evans

CONTENTS

CONTENTS

RENDEZVOUS IN VERACRUZ

1
THE PATH TO VERACRUZ

Dusk was falling that sultry June evening as Tommy Mallory screwed the engine cover plate back in place. He wiped a grease-stained hand across his face, leaving a smudge that only emphasized his blond good looks. But, at this moment, his customary smile was gone.

"I think the engine will go all right now, Nat, but I don't know how we're going to buy provisions or fuel. It took every penny to pay for that crankshaft. Do you think your dad would come through with some money?" And he looked down hopefully at his beautiful young wife.

Natalie shook her head without answering and lifted soft violet eyes to look across the water toward shore. The evening light bathed the sand with a golden glow and the squat whitewashed buildings seemed brushed with gold, too.

It was then that the muezzin began his chant, high on the minaret of the mosque. It was a soothing call for Mohammedans to observe their faith, but Natalie shivered a little. It was so alien and now she and Tommy were stranded here in Agadir, Morocco. They had spent every penny to buy the battered caïque, keeping only enough to make it back to Mexico. But they hadn't kept enough.

Natalie gently rubbed the smooth worn wood of the

deck. They had bought the boat in Crete, but it had been against her better judgment.

She had argued with Tommy, telling him it would take all of their money, that they wouldn't have enough to go back to school. He had swept away her objections. The boat was a steal, the best buy ever. They would sail it back to Mexico, sell it for a profit and go to school in clover.

Finally she had agreed because she knew it really should be an easy sail to Mexico in a boat that big and sturdy, but now they were stranded on the North African coast with only the first leg of the journey behind them and Mexico a long way to go.

Natalie shook her head again, then her bubbly ir- resistible smile surfaced. "I don't know what we'll do, Tommy, but there's no need to starve yet. We still have enough money for dinner at Mr. Stefanakos' café. Let's go eat."

Ever ready to play now and worry later, Tommy pulled her to her feet and together they jumped from the deck to the dock.

In the café, they found Mr. Stefanakos very interested in their plight, very sympathetic.

The Greek proprietor of the small waterfront café had been keenly interested in the two young Americans ever since their straggling arrival in port two weeks past, when they brought the caïque in under sail. He knew that they had eloped, that Natalie's parents had re- fused to help the couple, hoping this would influence Tommy to settle down and work, that Tommy managed off the income from a trust fund, that they were students at the University of the Americas in Mexico City.

He listened gravely, his dark eyes expressionless, as Tommy detailed their plight over a plate of octopi cooked in wine. By the time Tommy had finished his fifth glass

RENDEZVOUS IN VERACRUZ

of resinated wine, the proprietor knew just how broke and desperate the Mallorys were.

Tommy plunked down his wine glass and waved Mr. Stefanakos to a seat at their table. Then he leaned close to the café owner. "I'll tell you, sir, we are busted." He began to pull off his Swiss wrist watch. "Would you like to buy this so I can pay for our dinner tonight?"

The Greek shook his head.

"I'll have to wash dishes then," the blond American said dolefully.

Natalie smiled and opened her purse. "Don't worry, Mr. Stefanakos, we have enough to pay for dinner tonight. But Tommy is right, we don't have enough to go anywhere. I don't suppose there is a Traveler's Aid station in Agadir?" she asked, only half humorously.

Shadows were lengthening in the room. The candle light shifted and flickered, making the dark saturnine face of the Greek even more masklike than usual.

He turned his hooded eyes full on Natalie. "No," he said softly. "But perhaps I can help you."

Natalie stared at him, but she could read nothing in his dark lined face.

He stood. "When you finish dinner, perhaps you will have the goodness to join me in my office." He waved his hand toward a passageway angling off behind the bar. "And do not worry about dinner tonight. You are my guests." He bowed and left them.

"Hey, Nat, did you get that?" Tommy asked excitedly.

The girl nodded slowly. She didn't share Tommy's quick enthusiasm. What sort of work could she and Tommy do for a Greek café owner in a North African port?

Maura Kelly shaded her eyes from the brightness of the July sun and looked out over the glittering blue water of the bay of Acapulco. Without doubt it was one of the most beautiful views in the world, but she was getting bored with all of it, the view, swimming all day, dancing most of the night. Fun, but everything so much the same.

"Maura!"

She looked up at the glad cry and languidly waved. Rafael and Nicolas. Well, they were fun, but also so much the same, nice boys from nice backgrounds. How she would love to meet a really exciting man!

With a quick gesture, she swept down the sand castle and settled back on a towel, her flame-colored hair spreading out, vivid against the soft blue of the terrycloth.

When the boys dropped down beside her, she favored each with a warm smile. As they eagerly discussed the party planned for that evening and the marvelous fireworks scheduled by the American host, Maura contributed a casual word here and there. But to herself she was determinedly wishing the summer well gone. Surely something exciting would happen in the fall when school started again. Perhaps she would meet a man, a different sort of man . . . .

The sweat streamed down Luis Mendoza's face and back and legs. He stopped and tried to wipe his face clean but the handkerchief was soiled and dusty and the sweat smeared into his eyes and they began to burn.

He panted for breath and each draught of air seemed to burn his lungs more than the last. He wanted to give up and turn back. He was a fool to walk up into this hot and desolate country all on the chance that his informant was right and that Carlos was holed up in these hills.

He wanted to go back but he knew he couldn't. He might as well walk until he dropped and the August sun burned down and the vultures came, because he had nothing to walk back to. Not unless he could get the money.

He forced himself on, his legs leaden. He stumbled often, his body trembling from the unaccustomed strain. He had not walked this far in years.

When he reached the bent and twisted pine tree that he had been told to look for, he wearily sat down and rested his head on his knees. If the man he talked to had told him right, then the camp was only a half mile farther up the hill in a wide cleft hidden by tumbled boulders.

Only another half mile, his numbed mind urged, but he couldn't get up.

He heard nothing. The gun butt caught him between the shoulders without warning. He tumbled face down into the gritty hard dirt. When he managed to half rise, his face twisted with pain, the muzzle of the gun was jammed against his forehead.

His captor was only a boy, but his face was hard. He swung the rifle to point up the path, then prodded Luis again with the muzzle.

Trembling with fear and pain and exhaustion, Luis scrabbled to his feet and began to plod up the hill. But now he had hope. His captor must be one of Carlos' men.

The camp sentry met them at the rise and waved them on. He seemed to be expecting them. Luis realized dully that the man in the village must have sent warning about him. Of course he had. Carlos hadn't eluded the police and even the federal troops without the aid of men in each little village and small town.

Luis hesitated when the path ended at a rockslide. A huge mound of boulders loomed ahead. At the boy's impatient shove, he realized they had reached their goal. The camp lay beyond the boulders. Awkwardly he scrambled up among the huge chunks of rock and then he reached the other side and dropped down onto hard ground and looked about him.

The camp didn't amount to much. Five thatched-roof huts huddled close against the cliffside. He looked up and saw the bone-gray walls curve out then up sheer. The huts could not be seen from above—or attacked from above. The ragged mound of boulders, knocked loose in an earth slide, effectively concealed the huts from anyone climbing the hill.

Carlos had a good camp, but of course he would. For two years he had been the terror of the hills. Even an Army search party couldn't rout him out. Carlos Rodriguez, *El Jefe,* the bandit chief no one could catch.

Luis stopped and waited. Four or five bearded men in dusty khakis paused to watch him. A thickset Indian stopped polishing the inlaid silver on a saddle to stare unblinkingly at Luis' alien appearance. An older swarthy man dismissed Luis with a glance, spitting contemputuously over his shoulder before he returned to his whittling.

Dust eddied in the hot wind. Flies clung to a side of beef hanging from a tree limb. Luis began to wish he hadn't come.

The boy had disappeared into the farthest hut. Luis stood impatiently first on one foot, then the other, but it didn't take the boy long. He came out of the hut and motioned for Luis to come.

Luis walked past the watching men and his muscles tightened against their palpable hostility. His heart thudded. He stepped inside the hut as if it were sanctuary.

An oil lamp burned smokily on a makeshift table. Carlos sat behind it. He raised his sleek dark head and his mocking eyes flicked up and down Luis.

In his soft Spanish, the bandit chief said, "You do me great honor, Luis. What brings you to visit a humble peasant?"

But his voice was not humble. Carlos had never been humble. As a ragged, ill-fed orphan of the streets, his eyes had mocked the immaculate son of the rich *hacienda* owner—just as they mocked him now.

Luis rubbed the sweaty palms of his hands against his trouser legs, then wished he hadn't as a smile flickered on Carlos' face.

Luis managed a lopsided smile.

"I want to borrow sixty thousand *pesos,*" he said baldly.

"Borrow?" The bandit chief laughed a little. "This is no bank, Luis."

Luis walked up to the rickety desk and leaned over, spreading his hands wide on its top.

"But you have money, much money, and I must have sixty thousand *pesos.*" He heitated, then continued in a rush, "You know how rich my father is. And I am the only son. Someday I will have much money and I will pay you back. Double the amount. I wouldn't try to cheat you."

Again a smile flickered across the vivid face of the bandit chief. "I know that," and his eyes were contemptuous. "But all the banks know how rich your father is," he said softly. "They will loan you money."

"They would tell my father," Luis muttered.

"So?"

Luis' shoulders sagged. "He paid my debts once. He said if it ever happened again, he would disown me."

Carlos nodded. He had grown up in the valley. He did not need Luis to tell him that the old *señor* never broke a vow.

"Ignore your debt then," Carlos advised easily. "No one will press too hard a man who will someday be so rich."

Luis didn't look at Carlos. His hands, pressed so hard against the tabletop, trembled.

"I should have won," he said finally. "I have a good system and I *was* winning. And then a month ago, it all went wrong and the red came up every time."

"Roulette," Carlos said. He shook his head. "You have always been a fool, Luis."

Luis' handsome face twisted with fear. "They will kill

me if I don't pay! But if I go to my father—I might as well be dead."

The bandit shrugged. "Oh, one can live poor. I have managed." He studied Luis, the slender handsome face, the weak mouth. He could never succeed as a bandit, not as a man really. But something flickered in the dark intelligent eyes of the bandit.

"What are you doing these days, Luis? Aren't you studying at the National University?"

Puzzled, Luis nodded.

Carlos smiled sardonically. "And do you still have a way with women as you always did?"

Luis flushed a little. "What do you mean?"

"I mean that maybe we can make a deal. I will loan you the money if you will do some work for me. If you do it right, I may even forget the debt."

"Anything," Luis said quickly. "I'll do anything."

"There is a house in Mexico City where some girls live who are attending the University of the Americas. Can you become friendly with one of them?"

"Sure," Luis replied. "What's her name? Just give me her name."

Carlos shrugged. "It doesn't matter which one. The object is to gain entry to the house. Once you do that, I will send you further instructions."

"Anything you want, Carlos, just send the word," Luis said expansively, secure and happy with the money promised.

"Don't worry. I will."

Luis tucked the money and the address of *Señora* Alvarez in his pocket. He was ready to go. Then he paused. Free of his own fear, he looked at his old playmate with puzzled eyes.

"Why are you here?" he asked Carlos. "Why do you hide in the hills and rob the banks? I heard you were a great success in law school. You had a future ahead of you. Why have you come back to the hills and this?" He spread his arm wide in the dimly lit hut. "And I've heard that you only rob banks. You must have much money. Why don't you take it and leave the country and enjoy life?"

Carlos half smiled. "Wine, women and song, Luis. Is that what you suggest?"

Luis shrugged. "What else is there? But I guess you're just hanging on until you make a real killing."

The bandit chief's smile broadened and his eyes glinted with laughter.

"That's right," he said softly. "Until I make a real killing."

A delighted and delightful smile softened the grave reserve of Lin Prescott's face as the seat belt sign flashed to life on the bulkhead above her seat. Quickly she fastened the belt then twisted to look out the window.

The rugged countryside, splotched gray and green, slid past far below.

The loudspeaker gave a preliminary squeak then the voice of the hostess sounded loud and clear. She spoke in soft and liquid Spanish and Lin smiled happily again. Then the hostess repeated her message in English.

"We will be landing in Mexico City in fifteen minutes. The weather is clear and the temperature sixty-seven degrees. Please remain seated until the plane has come to a complete stop. Upon disembarking, you will need to clear Mexican immigration and customs."

As the stewardess closed with their altitude and flying time and an unexpectedly cheery wish for a happy holiday, Lin pressed her nose against the window and strained for her first view of the oldest and loveliest city of the Americas.

Abruptly the plane cleared the last of the mountains and far below, cupped in a valley 7,000 feet high, spread

Mexico City. And it was, Lin realized, a truly huge city. She knew it was home for six million people, but still she hadn't expected to see such a farflung dense mass of buildings.

As the plane lost altitude, she could see skyscrapers and hovels, narrow lanes and superhighways, and colors shading from white to beige to tawny gold.

The American girl took a deep breath to steady the rising surge of excitement within her. Her grand adventure was beginning. And she still couldn't believe it was actually happening.

She spared a glance at her fellow passengers, few of whom were registering any excitement at all. Some were American tourists, middle-aged and prosperous. Some were Mexican businessmen. She looked at them and felt sure that none had as much to look forward to as she, this beautiful September day. She wasn't landing for a short holiday or to end a routine business trip. Mexico City would be her home for the next nine months as she attended the University of the Americas. She couldn't restrain a slight feeling of superiority. In only a moment, the sleek jet would land and she would begin an entirely new life.

She snapped open her purse. Her American passport and smaller, stubbier Mexican student visa were safe in the side pocket alongside her packet of travelers' checks.

Pulling out her passport, she flipped to the page with her picture and a sober-faced Lin stared up at her. She smiled a little ruefully at the photograph. In it she didn't look at all glamorous, no matter how cosmopolitan she felt.

She closed the passport and dropped it back into her purse and her fingers brushed against a stiff white envelope—her letter of welcome from *Señora* Alvarez in whose home she would live. All of the University students roomed with families. Lin had chosen to live in a house which boarded eight students.

She could scarcely wait to meet the other students and to see her new home. She knew she would share a room with a junior, Maura Kelly. She had even received a gay note of welcome from Maura, assuring Lin that it would all be a ball.

The plane banked and curved, they were landing. Lin sat up straight, shut her purse and smiled. This was it.

After the jet, so swift in flight, had slowly trundled to its parking space, Lin waited impatiently for the line of travelers to move up the aisle to the exit. When she reached the ramp, she looked eagerly around before walking down.

The airport was small compared with many new ones in the United States, but a red carpet led from the edge of the runway into the airport. How was that, she thought, for traveling international style!

Once within, she took her place in one of the several lines leading to the Mexican officials' desks. It didn't take long. A glance at her passport and a quick stamping of her student visa and she was through.

She glanced around the long, wide waiting room and saw the luggage. As she fished for her claim tags, she felt a qualm. Families were greeting returned travelers with great emotion. Aunts and uncles and cousins embraced. Americans, mostly in pairs, quickly claimed their cases and began to leave. Soon the crowd of travelers and greeters dwindled until only Lin and two American couples remained. The girl looked anxiously about. *Señora* Alvarez was supposed to meet her.

Then Lin shrugged. If the *señora* didn't come, surely she was big enough to hire a taxi and go to her new home. Opening her purse, she pulled out the letter of welcome. The address was on *Prado Norte,* a street in the *Lomas de*

Chapultepec colonia, one of the District's loveliest suburbs.

As she reread the letter, a blithe voice inquired, "Are you Linda Prescott, by any chance?"

And she looked up into the bright blue eyes of one of the handsomest men she had ever seen. He ran a hand through thick blond hair and grinned engagingly.

"I'm sure sorry we're late. You are Linda, aren't you?"

"Yes," she said hastily.

"Glad we found you. I'm Tommy Mallory and this is my wife, Natalie."

Lin turned and said hello to the darkly beautiful girl at his side.

Natalie said warmly, "We are sorry to be late. The traffic hung us up. I know you were expecting *Señora* Alvarez, but she's gone to visit her daughter in Orizaba and we promised we would pick you up."

"It's awfully good of you," Lin said. "I'm very grateful you came. I was beginning to feel a little overwhelmed."

Natalie drew Lin's arm through her own and said reassuringly, "You've no idea how soon you will be running about Mexico City, feeling completely at home."

And everything did seem quite simple under the guidance of the ebullient Mallorys. In no time at all, Lin and her luggage were installed in the back seat of the couple's VW and they were roaring down a broad boulevard toward the heart of town.

Lin was delighted to learn that both the Mallorys were students at the University of the Americas.

"I used to room at *Señora* Alvarez'," Natalie explained. "Then when Tommy and I got married this spring, she took pity on our tiny income and let us rent part of the servants' quarters."

"How marvelous," Lin said. "I'm so glad we live at the same place."

She relaxed back into her seat, savoring the musky

nutlike smell of the city, and decided that life couldn't be better. To go to school in Mexico City, to meet students from all over the world, what could be more fun?

And she could tell that she was going to love the Mallorys.

It was October 12, the opening day of the racing season at the *Hipódromo de las Américas* in Mexico City. The crowd was festive and the horses behind the starting gate seemed to reflect the tension in the air. The first race began and a low growl of excitement burst from thousands of throats.

Juan Borja didn't protest when a man squeezed roughly in beside him at the crowded railing overlooking the track. Instead, Juan leaned farther over the rail and yelled encouragement to the horse now leading around the far turn.

"*Vaya, vaya!*" Juan waved his fist and thumped the railing and paid no attention to a hand thrust into his jacket pocket. In an instant the rough stranger was gone. Juan didn't turn his head.

An hour later, alone in his one-room apartment, Juan pulled a small wad of paper out of his jacket pocket and spread the note smooth. The writing was pinched but the message was clear.

"*El Jefe* expects a shipment of 'antiquities' in late October. Middleman is a student at the University of the Americas, name and nationality unknown, but perhaps a resident at *Prado Norte* 305."

Juan read the mesage twice then tore it into small bits. He watched the pieces burn in an ashtray. He stirred the charred remains until they flaked into ash.

Prado Norte 305. Now he had a starting point.

2
MAURA AND
LUIS

Lin shivered and pulled her robe a little tighter. Mexico City might have one of the world's finest climates but it certainly could be chilly on a rainy afternoon late in October. Particularly since none of the houses had central heating.

She plopped down her history book and pulled the little electric heater closer. She had bought it her second week in Mexico and she paid *Señora* Alvarez 60 extra *pesos* a month to run it, but, brother, was it worth it!

And then she smiled. Aren't you tough? she asked herself. Ruefully, she decided she wasn't. She did love her creature comforts. Thinking of such, she poured some bottled water into a tiny saucepan, tilted it precariously on top of the heater, waited until the water warmed, then dumped it into a cup with some instant coffee. And it couldn't be beaten in the best stateside dormitory.

Sipping the lukewarm brew, she picked up her book. Two paragraphs later she put it back down. Even upstairs in the bedroom, she could recognize the excited clatter of shoes coming up the tiled stairs. Maura was coming and coming fast. Wondering what great tale of joy or woe her exuberant roommate would have to impart, Lin began to smile in anticipation.

The door swung wide and slammed against the wall.

Her thick flame hair curling damply from the rain, Maura whisked off her scarf, dropped her raincoat on the floor and flung her arms wide.

"Darling, I've met him at last!"

"Who?" Lin inquired mildly. "The postman? If so, tell him I haven't received at least a half dozen letters lately."

"Of course not the postman!" Maura cried in disgust. "I have met a man," she continued dramatically. Waltzing to her twin bed, she collapsed onto it backwards and thrust her arms toward the ceiling. "A real live beautiful man. At last, after all the pale anemic youths I have dated!"

"A real man?" Lin asked dubiously. "I mean, how old is he?"

Maura pulled her pillow free from the spread and propped herself comfortably against the wall behind her bed.

She shrugged. "Oh, he's not so old. About twenty-two, I guess." She paused and her eyes gleamed. "He's the handsomest man I ever saw in my life."

"Where did you meet him?" Lin asked eagerly. "Out at school?"

Maura grinned mischievously, then asked, "You won't tell anyone, will you?"

Lin frowned. "Tell anybody what?"

"How I met my new beauty?"

Lin hesitated, then gave in. "Okay, I'll keep quiet. Come on, give."

"He was out at school," Maura said ingenuously. "I noticed him having coffee on the terrace and then he got on the same bus I did. He smiled at me twice but was I ever the demure young miss."

"Then what happened?" Lin asked.

Maura grinned again. "I decided to go on downtown. It was such a pretty afternoon."

"Oh yeah," Lin agreed. "Practically fine for seals with arctic training."

"Who minds a little rain with a man like that in tow?" Maura demanded. "Anyway, I got off at the Diana and so did he and we both caught the same bus into town. I went to Sanborn's on *Madero* and sat down at a table for two and ordered an ice cream soda."

She paused and let the silence expand dramatically.

"Come on, come on!" Lin pleaded.

Maura savored every last ounce of suspense, then breathed, "It was beautiful. He came up, leaned across the table and said, 'I'm sorry I'm late.' 'Late for what?' I asked. And he said, 'So many years late in meeting you.' "

Maura smiled, a thoroughly satisfied smile, then continued. "He sat down and we had the most marvelous talk. And I have a date with him tonight. We're going to the jai-lai games." She pushed up from her bed and moved to fling the wardrobe door wide. "I wonder whether I should wear my red jumper or do you think the corduroy culottes?"

Lin grimaced. "I think sackcloth and ashes would be more appropriate. Or maybe a well-cut hairshirt. Oh, Maura, how could you?"

The redhead pulled out the beige culottes, then shot an irritated look at her roommate. "Don't be such a heavy," she commanded. "It's perfectly all right. His name is Luis Mendoza and he's a student out at the National University. And besides, I saw him out at school."

"That doesn't mean a thing," Lin replied heatedly. "You haven't been properly introduced. He could tell you anything."

Maura rolled her eyes in disgust. "Good grief, I wouldn't have told you a thing about it if I'd known you would take it so hard."

Lin was silent for a moment, her gray eyes serious and

worried. She hesitated, then said firmly, "In our list of rules from the University, it said we should never, never accept a date with anyone to whom we hadn't been properly introduced. It just isn't done in Mexico."

Maura flushed, then shrugged. "Don't be so stuffy, little one. Old Maura can take care of herself. Don't forget, this is my third year at the University and I lived down here when my father was at the Embassy."

Lin capitulated. "Well, I suppose anybody who speaks Spanish as well as you do can handle most situations. Was he surprised at how fluent you are?"

Maura's mouth curved in a satisfied half-smile. "You have a lot to learn, love. Never, never let a Mexican man know how well you speak his language. They do like to help you out. I manage a few broken phrases and nothing more. It would surprise a half dozen boys I've dated if they knew my secret."

She laughed aloud. "I not only have gone to college here for three years and majored in Spanish, but my grandmother is a native of Madrid. Plus my dad was stationed at the Embassy here when I was in junior high. I can *hablo* with either a Castilian or a Mexico City accent, but only the tradesmen know it."

Lin joined in her laughter. "You are a devil. I'll remember your advice, but my Spanish is so bad right now that I don't have to fake it."

The rest of the afternoon passed in a flurry of getting Maura ready for her big date. True to her word, Lin didn't spill the facts when Maura told the other girls vaguely that she had met Luis out at school.

After dinner almost all of the girls managed to be downstairs in the common room reading and chatting when it was time for Luis to arrive.

And he really was something else! With his crisp black hair, flashing black eyes and lean good looks, he fascinated them all. And then he proceeded to charm them.

"I haven't seen as many beautiful girls since I went to UCLA," he said lightly. "And not even then."

As is usual with an educated Mexican, his English was flawless. He was also very kind about their halting Spanish. Lin was secretly amused to note that Maura's Spanish was the worst of the lot.

After the couple left, Mary Sisney pushed her horn rims up on her nose and moaned, "How does she do it? And so darned consistently. Almost every night there's some Latin lover just panting to take Maura out!"

Della Corey sadly picked up her anthropology text and said, "I guess it helps to be beautiful," but there was no envy on her plain little face.

"Maura's not only beautiful, she has what it takes," Barbara Evans chimed in. She paused then added ruefully, "I only wish I knew what that was."

"How can you complain, Barb?" Lin demanded. "Mike Rifkin absolutely haunts the house for you. I'll bet he's here tonight as usual."

"Yeah, there is that," Barb agreed. "And Mike's a nice guy, but what do we do? Study together! And look at Maura. Jai-lai tonight, it'll be the *Jacaranda* tomorrow night."

And Barbara was right. Every night Luis was there and every night when Maura got in the girls heard a dazzling report of the District's finest night spots and of Luis. Flowers arrived every afternoon. And Luis' sleek MC pulled up in front of the house every morning to give Maura a lift out to school, some 14 kilometers out the Toluca road.

"And that must be love," Mary told the other girls. "Look how far out of his way he goes. The National University is way southeast."

In less than a week, Luis became a familiar and accepted visitor at the house. Lin felt just a tinge of envy.

Wouldn't it be great to date someone like Luis! But she knew she would never meet anyone like that. Probably, she decided dismally, because she would just ignore anyone who tried to meet her at Sanborn's.

But Friday afternoon it was Lin who clattered excitedly up the stairs to burst like a whirlwind into their room.

"Maura, guess what?" she cried, her gray eyes sparkling.

"Let's see," the redhead mused teasingly, "I'll bet you got an A on your history quiz."

"Oh, that," Lin said in disgust, dismissing all her hours of study. "Yes, I did, but so what? No, I have some real news. A boy in English lit has asked me out."

"Great," Maura rejoiced. "Who is he?"

"Juan Borja. Do you know him? He's about five foot ten and he has sandy brown hair . . . ." Her words trailed off at Maura's frown.

The redhead nodded slowly. "I know who he is." She hesitated, then said, "I heard an odd story about him over coffee last month."

"What kind of story?" Lin asked slowly.

Maura took a cotton ball from the container on her dresser, sopped up some polish remover and began to swipe her nails with short firm strokes. She finished one hand before looking up to meet Lin's gaze.

"I was out on the terrace with George Hammond. You know him?" At Lin's nod, Maura continued, "Juan sat down a few tables away from us and George asked me if I knew him. I said yes. George shook his head and said, 'That Juan is one funny fellow.' Of course, I asked George what he meant.

"It turns out that George was down in Veracruz in September to go fishing with some friends. One night, it was a Friday, the boys planned to stay out on the boat all night. Well, George isn't much of a sailor and it was hot and muggy and generally miserable weather so he decided to stay on shore. He was drinking a beer at one of the sidewalk cafés on the *Plaza* when he heard someone running. A man plunged out from a side street and then George saw why he was running. Close behind him were a couple of toughs and one of them had a knife.

"The first guy stumbled and crashed into a table, knocking it and the dishes and the people all over the sidewalk. George was standing up by now and he saw the thug with the knife smiling and he had his arm up and he was getting ready to stab the guy who'd fallen down.

"George picked up his chair and threw it. It knocked down the man with the knife and then all of a sudden someone pinned George's arms from behind.

"It was the policeman, of course. And by the time everybody gathers around, all yelling and trying to tell it first, the tough guys are nowhere to be found. And when the whole mess of the table and the people eating dinner is sorted out and George is being acclaimed as a hero, the guy who was being chased gets up—and it's Juan!"

"Oh, Maura," Lin said skeptically.

"George swears it! Although, to be fair, the fellow denied he was Juan. He came up to George and very formally thanked him and George said, 'Juan, why's somebody chasing you with a knife?' And Juan looked right at him and told him he was mistaken, that his name was Tómas Andoni, and then he was gone."

"George was mistaken," Lin said firmly.

Maura shrugged. "All things are possible, but George sat next to Juan in anthropology all spring. He also played softball with him. And, to top it off, George asked around about Juan when he got back to school and nobody knows anything about him."

Lin frowned.

"Now you do have to admit that's strange," the red-head insisted. "All Mexicans have families, oodles and loads of family. And nobody knows where Juan is from or anything about him!"

Lin plumped down unhappily in a rickety wicker chair and plucked at a loose strand on the arm. Finally, she looked up appealingly at her roommate.

"I know you mean well, Maura, but I can't believe there is anything odd about Juan. We've had coffee on the terrace lots of times and we've talked about all kinds of things." She paused. "Never his family or anything like that, but books and what we like to do and what kind of life we want."

She rushed ahead, surer of her words now. "He's tremendously interested in English literature. That's one reason he's attending the University since most classes are taught in English. And he likes to ride and swim and play poker."

Maura's grin stopped her. Lin flushed.

The redhead reached out to touch Lin lightly on the arm. "I'm not really laughing at you. Don't be mad. But I love the idea he's a right guy because he likes to play poker."

A little unwillingly, Lin smiled, too. But she continued stubbornly, "He really is all right, Maura, I just know it."

"Okay," Maura said quickly and warmly. "Go out with him and have a wonderful time. You're a better judge of people than I am anyway. And forgive me for poking my long bony nose into your business."

Lin smiled in earnest at Maura's characterization of her slender and aristocratic nose.

Maura shook her head in mock resignation. "I am only admitting a truth that will come with age. You should see the long and bony nose of my grandmother."

And with that the afternoon slipped into the usual

Maura and Luis

frame of casual chatter and easy camaraderie. Before it seemed possible, shadows were lengthening and the girls began to dress for their dates.

Maura was in the communal bath down the hall with Lin waiting impatiently in a hall chair when the front door knocker sounded. Lin sat up straight as she heard the soft scurry of the maid's footsteps.

It had to be either Luis or Juan! The other girls either didn't have dates or had already left. But it shouldn't be either because it was still half an hour until eight o'clock.

Very quietly, Lin moved close to the head of the stairs and bent low to peer between the bannisters. She saw the flurry of Maria's long skirts as she turned toward the kitchen and then she saw Luis standing in the middle of the common room. Lin was just ready to retreat and alert Maura when she paused, puzzled by Luis' manner.

He was standing very still and the taut line of his shoulders reminded her of a painting that hung in her father's office. She had never liked the painting. It was of a black panther poised to leap, his muscles bunched, his eyes gleaming, a study in grace—and danger.

Luis' head moved slowly as he looked around the room. Then he stepped quietly, so quietly, into the hall and peered toward the kitchen wing. Lin knew the swinging door would be closed now, the maids readying their own meal.

The entrance hall light gleamed on Luis' upturned face as he lifted his head to look up the stairs. Lin stiffened, but he didn't see her in the darkness of the upper hall. She felt a quick rush of thankfulness that *Señora* Alvarez was so particular about the light bill. Lin was quite sure she wouldn't have liked Luis to see her watching him.

Luis glanced once more around the entrance hall. It lay quiet and empty. Satisfied now that he was alone and unobserved, he moved quickly into the common room and crossed to the ornately carved mantel above the stone fireplace. Again he glanced swiftly around, then in a hurried and furtive movement he pulled a cream-colored envelope from his breast pocket and thrust it beneath the slightly raised base of a bronze clock that sat on the mantel.

3
A VERY TALL TALE

Lin stayed in her tight crouch close to the bannisters and stared down in disbelief. Luis moved quickly away from the mantel and sat down in a rattan chair near the archway to the hall. His well-tailored legs were immobile, his hands relaxed upon the chair arms, but he couldn't keep his eyes away from the clock.

Behind her, Lin heard the preliminary rattle of the bathroom door. Maura would be coming out and Lin certainly didn't want Luis to hear her demanding in her clear audible voice what Lin was doing on the floor by the stairs.

Swiftly Lin scooted backward until she was out of sight from below, then she popped to her feet and rushed to the bathroom, almost colliding with Maura as she pushed open the door.

"Luis is here," Lin whispered.

"Already?" Maura asked. "He's early." She walked to the head of the stairs. Drawing her robe close, she leaned over and called, "Be down in a minute, Luis."

"I would wait for you forever," the easy call came, but Lin's heart didn't pitty-pat this time. A three-year-old would grasp that there had been something a little odd in the scene she had witnessed.

She followed Maura into their room and closed the door

RENDEZVOUS IN VERACRUZ

tight. Her roommate began to pull a silvertoned sheath dress over her head.

"Zip me up, Lin, that's a lamb."

Automatically Lin stepped close and began to zip, even as she spoke. "Listen, Maura, Luis did something very strange downstairs."

All zipped, Maura moved away to lean close to the mirror over the dresser. As she expertly wielded her lipstick brush, she murmured, "What, darling? Did he chin himself from the chandelier or talk to an invisible goose?"

"He put an envelope under the bronze clock on the mantel in the comon room," Lin said flatly.

Maura's hand stopped in midstroke. She turned and faced Lin.

"He did what?"

"He took an envelope out of his breast pocket, looked around to make sure nobody was watching him, then stuck it under the clock."

Maura looked at Lin's clear serious gray eyes, her sturdy sensitive face.

"You aren't kidding, are you?"

Lin shook her head.

"How very peculiar," Maura said softly.

"That's exactly the thought that occurred to me," Lin said drily. "Are you going to go out with him?"

Maura stood very still. Slowly a sardonic smile curved her lips. "The Mystery of the Message. I think I shall have a great deal of fun tonight."

Lin frowned. Behind Maura's laughter she heard a thin edge of anger.

"I don't think I would, really, Maura. No one up to any good goes around hiding letters under clocks."

Maura swept to the wardrobe and pulled out a short mink jacket. "You have something there, old buddy. But no one dates me only to gain entrée to someone else's house either—and gets off scot-free."

Lin looked stricken. "You think he did that? Dated you just to be able to come into the house? But why should anyone? I mean, a houseful of girls and *Señora* Alvarez. Why would anyone do that?"

"I don't know now, darling. But I will before the evening is over."

And Maura moved purposefully out of the room, more beautiful even than usual, her dark eyes glinting with the light of anger, her hair a burnished red.

Lin almost moved after her. But what good would that do? Maura had made up her mind. Why had she ever told her? But, of course, she had to. And then she heard the knocker sound downstairs. Dear heaven, that would be Juan, her first real date, and here she stood in a scruffy chenille bathrobe.

She rushed out to the hall, called down that she would be only a minute and she wasn't more than five. As she clattered breathlessly down the stairs, he grinned, "Slow down. Your roommate's already apologized to me. She said she monopolized the bath and made you late. But there's no need to hurry, we have the whole evening before us."

Lin skidded to a stop on the bottom step and held out her hand to him. Before this evening, she had contrasted him with Luis and admitted to herself that Luis was much the handsomer. But tonight she looked at his stocky powerful frame, his candid blue eyes and his plain sturdy face, and he looked wonderful.

"I'm so glad to see you," she cried.

A little startled but pleased at her warmth, he replied, "And I am very glad to see you, *señorita*."

And then they were off, hand in hand. They strolled through the chill crisp night to *Reforma* and hailed a cruising taxi. Traffic curved and whirled on that beautiful boulevard, the car lights illuminating briefly in turn the intricate black iron grilles of old balconies, the bright glass sheen of modern skyscrapers, sleekly dressed couples sauntering at ease on the wide flagstoned sidewalks, a raggedly dressed young Indian mother clutching a baby, one hand out-thrust for a peso. It was all there on this loveliest street, the beauty and the glory and the sadness of Mexico.

As their taxi cut from one lane to another, fighting for an inch here, a foot there, Lin stared out the window. Where now in this huge city was Maura? And was she safe?

"You're very quiet," Juan remarked.

She turned to him with a quick smile. "The city can overwhelm you sometimes." Determined not to ruin this evening, she swung away from the topic. "What are we going to do tonight?"

"I thought we might have dinner at the *Villa Fontana*. Would you like that?"

"Like it!" Her gray eyes shining, she exclaimed, "That would be fabulous! I've heard so much about it."

And it was all that she had heard and more, the international cuisine, the hauntingly lovely music of the violins, the cosmopolitan diners. She stopped midway through her filet mignon to look happily around the terrace. She could hear snatches of French and the guttural bark of German and, of course, the rattly English of Americans. The lights began to dim and the waiters stood back. It was time again for the twelve violinists. As the music soared, she turned serious gray eyes toward Juan and spoke softly.

"I want to thank you for this evening. This is the most glamorous place I've ever been. I'm from a little town in Missouri and, believe me, they have nothing like the *Villa Fontana* there."

"I'm glad you like it. But there is much more to Mexico than sophisticated supper clubs." He hesitated, then asked with a shadow in his eyes, "The girls who live at your house, have many of them traveled widely in Mexico?"

Lin shook her head. "Nobody except Maura, really. Oh, Barbara and Jane have been to Cuernavaca and I think Mitzi's gone to Taxco, but Maura is the only one who really knows the country. I mean, as much as a foreigner can."

"Is Maura from Missouri, too?"

Lin grinned. "Nope. She's from Albuquerque, N.M., but she's lived all over the world. Her dad is in the diplomatic service. She loved it when he was stationed down here. She's really fun. I've never known anyone like her." Then she paused and a little frown drew her brows together.

"What's wrong?" Juan asked quickly.

She looked up and sighed. "Do you mind if I tell you? I've tried not to think about it all evening, but Juan, I'm worried!"

"Tell me," he encouraged.

Quickly she described Luis' arrival and his odd behavior and the note thrust under the clock and Maura's anger and her determination to find out what was going on.

"Do you see why it worries me?" Lin asked. "I mean, it was such a strange thing to do!"

"I can see," he said slowly. He was quiet for a moment, his face blank, but his thoughts quick and clear.

"How long has she known him?"

"Just a week," the girl said unhappily. "And it has bothered me from the first. She wasn't properly introduced."

Juan looked at her, his face unreadable. "It is very important to observe the proprieties. She should not have gone with him tonight."

When he saw the quick distress on Lin's face, he reached across the table to touch her hand. "Don't be worried. I didn't mean she was in danger. I only mean it is most foolish to date without an introduction."

He hesitated, then said urgently, "If I were you, Lin, I would be very discreet about the message under the clock."

"Discreet?" she repeated, puzzled.

He nodded and smiled. "It is all right to have told me. I won't repeat it. But hasn't the most likely explanation occurred to you?"

She stared at him in surprise. "The likeliest explanation! I think you're fantastic if you can suggest any explanation at all, much less a likely one!"

His smile broadened. "Luis is a very definite type, isn't he? I can't imagine him writing many letters, but I can certainly see him dashing off love letters without any difficulty."

"Love letters! But he's dating Maura . . . ." Her voice trailed off.

"Exactly," he said, "but it would be like him to write to someone else."

Lin frowned and thought. "I can't imagine him knowing anyone else in the house. I mean, none of the girls are nearly as beautiful as Maura."

"There is Mrs. Mallory," Juan suggested.

"Oh, Natalie wouldn't do something like that!" Lin exclaimed. "At least, I don't think so." And then she looked, her eyes puzzled, at Juan. "Do you know Natalie?"

Juan shook his head. "Not really. She was a beauty queen last year. And she is very beautiful."

Lin frowned. "I can't imagine Natalie receiving love letters from Luis."

The Mexican shrugged. "I don't say this is so, but it is possible. Now, let's not worry any more about all this. It can't be anything serious. And I wouldn't worry about your roommate. She sounds very—capable."

If a problem shared is not a problem solved, it was certainly a worry lessened as far as Lin was concerned.

In the glamorous and civilized restaurant, the odd incident no longer seemed so threatening and the picture of a panther poised to leap faded from Lin's mind.

As Juan leaned close and began to describe the Great Pyramids north of the District and the excavations underway there, all thoughts of Maura slipped away from Lin. A little later when he excused himself with a smile, Lin didn't associate his absence with her revelations about Luis and the note.

Once off the terrace, Juan skirted through the main dining room toward the bar. He found the headwaiter and with a flourish of *pesos* received permission to use the telephone in the office. As he dialed, his fingers trembled a little with excitement. When the receiver was lifted on the other end, he spoke briefly and crisply, "This is Red Four calling about Operation Starfish. Probable contact made about the antiquities by one Luis Mendoza, about twenty-three, possibly a student at National University. Will report again tomorrow."

He hung up and hurried back to Lin. He hoped her roommate was not being foolish, but he shrugged away the thought. A foolish American girl was no concern of his.

". . . and so I paid him sixty *pesos* to take the exam for me," Luis continued. "It's simple when a class is that big. Then my father sent me a check for a hundred and twenty *pesos* for passing this semester." Luis leaned back in the low chair, a pleased smile on his face. "Sixty *pesos* clear profit and no study in the bargain."

Maura leaned across the cocktail table to murmur, "I think it's marvelous how clever you are."

He looked into her admiring brown eyes and his smile widened.

Maura thought it a singularly smug and self-satisfied smile. She wondered now how she had ever thought him so handsome. Her anger had destroyed his romantic image as effectively as an acid bath, but the smile she gave him was as warm and gay as when they first had met.

Abruptly, she looked away to conceal a quick flicker of disdain. As her gaze steadied, she was gripped once again by the magical sweep of lights so far below. In the dim and intimate dinner club on the 41st floor of the *Latino Americano* Building, every table offered a magnificent view of the District. Stretching away on all sides lay the city, a moving sea of color and form, a mosaic of light.

Maura spread out her hand. "Look at it, Luis. Isn't it fabulous? And just think of all the exciting and mysterious things that are happening in this city tonight."

He shrugged. "I guess so."

"There are always mysteries everywhere," she continued, her voice light. Her tone didn't alter when she added, "Such as the mystery of the note hidden under the bronze clock tonight."

His hand froze halfway to his glass. The smile slipped from his face and his eyes fastened on her as if he couldn't believe what he had heard.

Silence wrapped itself around their table.

Maura picked up her glass and her smile didn't waver.

She sipped at her drink and reached for a handful of *pepitas*. Finally, she shrugged. "Cat have your tongue, Luis?"

"What are you talking about?" he asked hoarsely.

"I'm talking about your odd postal system," she said easily. "Are you making dates with one of the other girls?"

She could tell that this solution appealed to him. He almost spoke and then he stopped. She could sense his thoughts. If he admitted to making dates with one of the other girls, she would have nothing further to do with him. And, for some reason, it was important to him that Maura date him.

He shook his head slightly and bent across the table. "Of course not, *querida mía*. Never would I do that. It is a different kind of matter, entirely." He turned and waved down the waiter. "Come on," he said urgently, "let's get out of here and I'll tell you all about it."

"Fine," she said agreeably, but her eyes narrowed speculatively.

As Luis laid a pile of *pesos* on the bill tray, she considered her position. She had stumbled into something, all right, and it could be something dangerous. But she was sure she could handle Luis.

When they reached the sidewalk, Maura pulled her jacket tight around her shoulders and resisted Luis' insistent pressure on her elbow.

"Where are we going?" she asked.

"We can talk at my apartment . . . ," he began.

Maura stopped short on the sidewalk.

"Your apartment?" she repeated. "No, thanks. That's the quickest way I know to be expelled from the University. Look, let's walk along and talk. Nobody will hear us."

"This is very confidential," he said reluctantly.

Maura looked up at him and she knew he was trying to gain time. He hadn't decided what lie to tell her. So she really had stumbled into something big! Now was the moment to convince him that she was a female fool.

Linking arms with him, she breathed, "Oh, I won't tell anyone, Luis! Why I know it must be something very important and mysterious and exciting. Do tell me all about it."

'Well, there isn't much to tell," he said and paused.

"Yes," she encouraged.

"You see, I'm a kind of courier."

"A courier," she said breathlessly.

"Yes," he said more emphatically. "I'm a courier and my job was to put the message under the clock."

She looked up at him expectantly. "But why?"

"I can't tell you," he replied. Then he continued strongly, "Don't you see, it's all very secret."

"But what in the world could involve one of the girls at the house or the *señora* that could call for leaving secret messages?" she asked sharply.

He stopped on the sidewalk and drew her off the pavement to the shadow of a huge palm. He looked up and down the street, then dropped his voice and said dramatically. "It is for the honor of Mexico, Maura. That is all I can tell you. And I know that as my friend and as a vistor in this country you would do nothing to interfere."

He waited anxiously for her reply.

And in a moment she did respond. "Luis," she trilled, "that's wonderful. Just tell me how I can help you. Perhaps I can pass the messages on."

He gripped her arm. "No, I wouldn't ask it of you. But you can help by telling no one of this."

"Oh, don't worry. I won't tell a soul. Don't worry about that at all."

She heard his quick sigh of relief. And then he took her arm and was urging her up the street at a fast clip. "Enough of these serious things," he said, his voice gay. "Let's go to *Las Catacumbes*. You'll love it."

Maura laughed and chattered and charmed throughout their visit in the dingy spook-infested bar, but her mind was tugging and pulling at her mystery.

She didn't believe a word Luis had said.

4
EASY AS YOU PLEASE

"I should think it would burst!" Lin cried with a laugh.

"What?" Juan asked.

"The Park, silly," and the girl spread her hand. "It couldn't hold another person."

Juan laughed then, too. "Of course it can. There's always room for more at *Chapultepec*. It is one of the biggest parks in the world."

On this Sunday afternoon, it seemed to Lin as if all of Mexico must be in *Chapultepec*. Brawny teenagers played soccer. Families picnicked with everyone present from the great-grandmother to the tiniest baby. And young lovers managed to walk dreamily even when squeezing past groups of children on the paths.

Lin and Juan tried out the pedal boats in the large lake in New *Chapultepec*. They shared pepper-sprinkled corn cobs with ducks in the zoo and took a ride on the children's train. They joined a tour of the hilltop Castle that had been home for Maximilian and Carlotta during their short rule of Mexico one hundred years earlier.

Shadows were lengthening as they sat at a tiny table outside a kiosk and devoured a plateful of *tacos*. Lin smiled in contentment.

"I seem always to be thanking you, Juan, for a wonderful experience. But today has been fine. I don't know when I've had such fun."

He smiled. "We will come again many times. We have scarcely begun to explore *Chapultepec*. Next Sunday we'll go to the Anthropology Museum. It is the finest in the world."

"That sounds grand," she replied. She gazed across the lake, still full of ill-managed rowboats, and breathed a sigh of pure happiness.

He looked at her profile and admired the soft glow of her skin in the sunlight. Then his eyes narrowed. But when she looked around at him, his smile returned. They sat in companionable silence until he said casually, negligently, "I forgot to ask you about your roommate. I suppose she did make it home okay last night?"

"About two in the morning," Lin replied drily. "I waited up for her. Pacing the floor, to be honest. And when she swept in as bright as a new penny, I didn't know whether to laugh or cry."

"Then Luis must have soothed her with some sort of explanation," Juan said.

Lin shrugged. "Not really, but Maura is a stubborn devil. He told her some fishy story about being a courier." At Juan's look of surprise, she said, "You know, like a spy of some sort. And all for the glory of Mexico. Frankly, he must think Maura's pretty stupid. Of course, that's what she wanted him to think. But she says she'll play his little game until she gets to the bottom of it."

"And what does Maura think could be the reason for Luis leaving secret messages in *Señora* Alvarez' house?" Juan asked quietly.

"Good grief, I don't know!" Lin exclaimed. "That's all she would say. I told her she was some kind of nut to have anything more to do with him so she won't discuss it anymore. But knowing Maura, she'll keep after it."

"Has she seen him since last night?" the boy asked.

"No, and I don't think she will until Tuesday. He especially said he would be by to take her out to the University Tuesday morning. And, since he always comes inside to pick her up, Maura's betting he plans to slip a note under the clock then. But Maura's not taking any chances. She hasn't moved out of the common room except to eat and sleep. She's watching that clock like a hawk."

"Tuesday," Juan repeated slowly.

Tuesday morning Maura passed up her usual third cup of coffee to clatter up the stairs a full half hour ahead of her schedule.

Lin watched her go with a troubled frown. She speared another slice of papaya but put it down half eaten and pushed back her chair.

She too hurried up the stairs but at the top she hesitated. She had already made it clear that she thought Maura was being foolish and it hadn't done a bit of good. Maybe she should mind her own business. After all, she was scarcely her roommate's keeper. She half turned to go back downstairs, then whirled around and walked swiftly into their room.

Maura was belting her raincoat as Lin came in.

"What are you up to, Maura? Luis doesn't come until eight to pick you up."

The redhead answered obliquely. "That's right. And why do you suppose he's coming?"

Lin sighed. "At this point, I don't have any idea. Maybe it's because he likes you."

Maura's lips curled. "Yeah. You bet. No, I think my old buddy intends to use his quaint postal system again."

"So why hurry?"

"Because if he comes to pick me up and plants a note under the clock I can't very well waltz up and pull it out again. And you can bet his correspondent will retrieve it before I get home."

Lin frowned. "Look, if you really think so and if you think it's important to find out what's going on, I could hang around and get the note after you leave."

Maura slowly shook her head. "You are a trooper to volunteer, but I don't want you mixed up in it. This is my problem. And I have a plan."

"I don't like it," Lin said abruptly. "I don't think you should get involved any further. Please, Maura."

"Don't worry about me," Maura replied. "I'm not stupid. And I wouldn't trust Luis with a silver spoon shackled to a German shepherd."

And with that she was gone.

Lin sighed, pulled on her raincoat and followed at a leisurely pace. As she walked slowly up *Prado Norte* toward *Reforma* and the bus, she worried.

Maura was breathless but prepared when she reached *Reforma*. She watched the oncoming traffic, ready to hail Luis. If he really did have another message to deliver, then her plan might work. And if it did, she wouldn't be long in knowing just what kind of strange game he was playing.

For an instant, she wondered if she should. And then she shook the thought away. She just couldn't buy the Secret Sam bit. Whatever Luis might be, and she could imagine a number of possibilities, she didn't think he could possibly be a Mexican secret agent. Not Luis.

And then she caught a glimpse of the MG cutting in front of a taxi and she began to wave—and she tried to look as worried and upset as possible.

Luis saw her and swerved toward the curb. As the car slid to a stop, Maura wrenched open the door, scrambled in and huddled down on the seat.

"Quick," she commanded. "Drive on."

He shoved the stick into low and the small car zoomed ahead.

"What's wrong?" he demanded, his hands tense on the wheel.

"Oh Luis, someone must be on to you!"

"What do you mean?" he asked harshly.

He was scared, she saw with quick and secret satisfaction. Now to pour it on.

"Two men are watching the house," she continued breathlessly. "There is a brown sedan parked up the street. It was there all day yesterday and it was back at seven this morning. And I'm just sure they are watching our house."

A muscle twitched in Luis' jaw. His right hand fell from the wheel to grip a small attaché case on the car seat between them.

"Are you sure?" he asked.

"Yes," she replied definitely. "I started to tell *Señora* Alavarez, but then I didn't because I didn't know who you were leaving the message for and . . . ."

He jerked his head and stared at Maura. "Did you tell anyone about the message?" His hand flashed across the seat to clutch her wrist. "Did you?"

"Luis, you're hurting me!" she cried.

The pressure eased on her wrist.

"Tell me. At once," he ordered and he was the dominant Mexican male shorn of any gallant pretense.

"Of course not," she replied angrily. "I promised. Besides, I wouldn't do anything to jeopardize your work. Oh Luis, do you suppose there is an enemy agent in the house?" she asked ingenuously.

For a moment, his eyes were blank. "Enemy agent?" he repeated. And then his voice deepened, "That must be it. I have been betrayed."

"Oh, Luis," she cried sympathetically, wondering as

she did if she were laying it on too thickly, but his quick glance betrayed only worry, not suspicion.

Without warning he cut across traffic and swerved off onto a side street. Pulling up under the shade of mimosa, he stopped the car and turned to her.

"I need your help. Mexico needs your help," he said earnestly.

"Oh Luis, I'll do anything!"

He grasped her hands and smiled tenderly—but his eyes were worried and calculating.

"It isn't much to ask. I want you to put a message under the clock." He paused and was very quiet for a moment. "I must add to the message."

He drew the attaché case to him and pulled out a cream-colored envelope and a small note pad. He pulled a sheet loose, wrote swiftly, then folded it and thrust it inside the envelope.

Again he paused and stared down at the envelope, his face creased in thought.

She reached out, but he didn't relinquish it.

"It will be simple. I will take you to within a block of the house. You can walk there, put the note under the clock and be back at the car within only a few minutes. Four minutes at the most."

She looked steadily at him. He was trying to make sure that she had no time to open and read the letter. Well, let him take his pains for all the good that would do.

"Okay," she said equably. And she again held out her hand for the letter.

Luis handed it to her. And then the MG roared to life. When they were a block from the house, he pulled in by the curb, and leaned across to open the door. As she stepped out, he said softly, "Be very quick."

"I shall."

She could feel his eyes on her back as she walked

Easy As You Please

swiftly up the sidewalk. She passed an Indian who had set up a little portable shoe shop beneath a weeping willow tree and exchanged a graceful greeting, but, as she turned the corner, her pace quickened to a run. She streaked past the stone walls and iron fences that lined the sidewalks, insuring each home its privacy. A maid unlocking a gate to lead two small children out looked up in surprise, but Maura's run didn't slacken.

The *señora's* house was midway up the block. During the daytime, the iron gate was never locked, only shut. Maura pushed it open with a clang and rushed up the flagstone steps to the door.

Once in the hall, she paused only long enough to see that no one was about. She could hear the soft voices of the cook and the maids in the kitchen, but the rest of the house lay silent. She hurried upstairs, pulled the door shut and crossed to her desk. Swiftly she rummaged through her stationery. No cream-colored envelopes. She shrugged, snatched up a plain white one, folded two sheets of blank paper, stuffed them inside, licked the flap and gummed it down.

She looked at the envelope Luis had given her. Should she hide it here? No, she couldn't possibly wait that long to read it. She undid her raincoat, tucked the envelope inside the waistband of her skirt, then buttoned her cardigan. With her raincoat fastened, Luis wouldn't see the small bulge.

She must hurry. Time was running out. She clattered down the stairs, pausing only long enough to slide the bogus envelope under the clock, then she was out the door and running hard.

Maura slowed to a walk as she neared the corner and her breath came evenly by the time she reached the MG.

"All done," she said brightly as she slid onto the seat. "Now be a dear and whisk me out to school or I'll be late for my nine o'clock."

"You put the envelope beneath the bronze clock?"

"Yes, of course. I did just what you asked. Now, come on, Luis. If we don't get started, I'll be late and Mr. Simmons hates for anyone to come to class after he starts lecturing. He snarls!"

Luis managed a faint smile, but it didn't reach his eyes. He regarded her steadily for another long moment, then he flicked on the ignition and they were off. All the way out the curving, narrow blacktop to the University, Maura chattered. Luis answered her shortly. He wasn't attempting to charm this morning.

Luis pulled in behind the school bus that was letting off students at the archway that framed the entrance to the campus. Maura was out of the car almost before it stopped. She called out over her shoulder, "I believe I'll make it. Thanks so much."

She darted through the archway and hurried up the flagstone walk. She risked one quick glance behind her, but Luis hadn't followed. Instead of mounting the stone steps toward the stuccoed class buildings, she veered to her left and walked into the three-story Administration Building.

Cutting through the small cafeteria, she walked out onto the terrace and again bore left. She followed the uneven stone steps down a long flight and came out on the narrow road that bordered the ravine behind the University. Her goal was a small two-storied building perched on the edge of the ravine, the office of the campus newspaper. She was hoping that it would be deserted as it often was so early in the day.

She opened the door very quietly and walked softly down the wooden steps until she could see the whole of the newsroom and the glistening green view of the ravine through the ceiling high windows. No voice lifted in greeting. The office was empty.

Maura sat down in a hard wooden chair and simply

relaxed. It was the first time all morning that she had felt safe. But she didn't rest long.

Pulling the cream-colored envelope from her waistband, she balanced it in her hand for a moment. Her mouth twisted a little. She was going to be embarrassed indeed if this did turn out to be a love letter. And she was going to be in a pile of trouble if it contained some sort of classified information concerning the Mexican government.

Then her lovely mouth hardened. No matter what it was, she was going to know. No one would date her as a means to an end and not rue the day.

She picked up a ruler and swiftly slit open the envelope. She pulled out the folded note that Luis had added in the car, another folded sheet that matched the cream-colored envelope, and a thick packet of American bills.

First she opened the folded paper that matched the envelope. The message read simply: 20°42′ N, 96°15′ W. 2400 hours, 25 October. Password—Do you like fish? The answer will be—Yes, especially the fish of the hills.

It was a very interesting message in several respects, not the least being that it was written in English. She hadn't believed Luis when he claimed to be a liaison agent to *Señora* Alvarez, but the message clinched it. No one would give the *señora* a password in English.

And then she picked up the note Luis had scrawled in the car. She smiled grimly as she read the words on the outside of the sheet: Tommy, Deliver this map with the shipment.

So Tommy Mallory was the fox in the chicken coop. It was he for whom the cryptic password was intended. It was Tommy who would make the midnight rendezvous.

It would be nice if she knew why.

Impatiently, she flipped open the added note. A map, all right, but the scrawled lines with their compass directions and mileage didn't mean much to her. She frowned

RENDEZVOUS IN VERACRUZ

and looked at the hand-drawn map. A bit of coastline, apparently. The map led inland and started at 20°42′ N, 96°15′ W.

And she still hadn't any glimmer why.

She picked up the thick packet of American bills. Money in it for Tommy or for somebody. She pulled off the rubber band and held up the top bill. She blinked and hastily riffled through the handful of bills she held.

"Oh, my," she said softly. She counted the bills. An even one hundred of them. Each worth $1,000. "Oh my," she said again. And then she laughed aloud. One hundred thousand dollars! She had heisted one hundred thousand dollars just as easy as you please. She wondered how Luis would like them apples! And then her smile faded. It did have its amusing aspects, but she doubted if Luis or whoever employed him would find it all that funny. In fact, she might be topping somebody's hate list right at this minute.

Maura leaned back in her chair and thought. In a moment, she picked up a gray sheet of copy paper, wrote swiftly in her firm clear hand, folded the note twice and wrote Lin's name on the back.

She put the cream-colored envelope with its contents into her raincoat pocket. From the other pocket she pulled out a black scarf which she wrapped around her head until not a telltale red hair showed, and then she slipped quietly out of the Journalism Building.

5

"MONEY, BABY, MONEY!"

Tommy Mallory bounded up the stone steps leading to the small apartment above the garage and quarters behind the Alvarez' home.

As he burst through the door, he pulled a white envelope out of his jacket pocket. He threw the envelope up in the air then caught it.

"This is it, Nat. Our passport to life and ease for a long time to come."

"Hush, Tommy," she urged. "Don't shout it to the world. I still wonder what we are mixed up in."

Tommy bent over to kiss the top of his wife's head. "Money, baby, money!"

Exuberantly, he ripped open the envelope and pulled out the folded sheets. He spread them open and the smile faded from his face. He stared in disbelief at the unmarked pages. He shook the envelope, then turned over the two sheets of paper.

"Nothing," he said blankly. "No message. No money. What kind of deal is this?"

Natalie leaned across the table and took the envelope and papers from him. She stretched the envelope wide and poked an exploring finger within. Then she studied the blank paper.

"Disappearing ink?" she suggested.

Tommy just looked at her.

She shrugged. "What now, lieutenant? I have a feeling that Mr. Stefanakos isn't going to like it awfully much if we rendezvous with the freighter and we don't have a pocketful of money."

Tommy shoved a hand through his unruly blond hair. "Well, he certainly can't blame us! The money was supposed to be under the clock."

"I knew it wouldn't be that simple," she said slowly. "It's too much money. Tommy, what are we going to do?"

He reached in his hip pocket and pulled out his billfold. Opening it, he withdrew a pink slip. "I have a number. I'm not supposed to use it except for an emergency."

"This should qualify," she said drily.

Lin carried her coffee cup and doughnut out of the lunchroom and settled down on the terrace in a comfortable webbed chair. It was almost deserted since most students had nine o'clocks.

She drank her coffee slowly, savoring each mouthful as it warmed her against the chill crisp morning. She ate her doughnut slowly too, enjoying the quiet and ease, in no hurry to set to work. It was tempting to daydream and watch the frosty cone of Mount *Popocatépetl* glimmering in the pale sunlight. She would miss the terrace and the beautiful view of the rugged country-side when the University moved to its new campus in Pueblo, but she had heard that the old colonial town was one of the most beautiful in Mexico so she would probably love it, too. With a final lingering glance at the old volcano, Lin began to study in earnest. In only two weeks, midterms began.

She was immersed in her book, oblivious both to the gradual filling of the chairs on the cement terrace and the beauty of the rugged countryside beyond the ravine, when someone tapped her on the shoulder.

Her mind tuned to the rolling cadence of Kipling's verse, she looked up blankly at first, then smiled at Della and snapped shut her book.

"Hi pal, join me in a cup."

Della shook her head and pushed her glasses up on her nose. "Wish I could, but I have to work in the library and I'm running late." She thrust a folded note in Lin's hand. "This is just Della's Delivery Service."

"What?" Lin asked.

"Personal post," Della replied. "It's a note from your roommate. I ran into her down by the J Building and she asked me to deliver it."

"Life with Maura is never dull," Lin said with a smile. "Thanks, Della."

"*Por nada*," the girl replied as she turned and hurried toward the lunchroom.

Lin unfolded the sheet. The words leaped up at her.

"Lin, I've landed in a jam and, like a good girl should, I'm going to hotfoot it to the Embassy. Our note hiding pal is apparently hooked up in something rather big league. I imagine the Embassy will want to talk to you, too, so please hover by the phone in the J office around 11 o'clock. I'll call then. And, if anybody asks, like Luis for instance, you haven't seen me since breakfast. M."

Lin read the note again and yet once again. She glanced down at her watch. Five minutes until ten. An hour to go. She was torn between irritation and worry. Why had Maura been so cryptic? What had she stumbled onto and why hadn't she said more in the note? And what did she mean by a jam? Was she in any sort of danger? Lin looked again at her watch but only a minute had passed. She quickly stood up, then sat down again. There wasn't anything she could do right now. She might as well go to class. Perhaps it would make the hour pass more quickly.

Maura carefully checked around the edge of the archway. No sign of Luis. Nowhere did she see the MG or, for that matter, anyone who looked out of place. There were only a few students milling about. The ten o'clock bus into town was never crowded. Maura waited until the last minute; then, after one more hasty inspection, she darted aboard the tomato-red school bus and hunched down in the seat. She held up her colonial history book to mask her face. With her hair and face hidden, Luis wouldn't recognize her even if he did see the bus. But she didn't breathe deeply until the bus was on its headlong way up the narrow curving highway toward town.

It seemed forever before the bus reached the Diana, the golden-hued statue of the huntress on the glorieta that marks the entrance to *Chapultepec* Park. This was the end of the line for the bus. Now it would swing about for the return trip to the University.

Maura debarked hard on the heels of three chattering coeds, then she walked swiftly until she was swept up in the unending stream of pedestrians. She hurried with her head bent and her hands pushed hard into the pockets of her raincoat. It wasn't until she was a block beyond the Diana that she drew off the sidewalk to look carefully around. And then she leaned against the rough bark of a palm and breathed deeply. No one was paying the slightest attention to her. For an instant, her cheeks flushed and she wondered if she was being a fool.

Luis, after all, couldn't be everywhere at once. Perhaps she was ridiculous even to think he was hunting for her. That comforting thought withered and died the instant it was born. He would be hunting, all right. He and whoever was behind him. People don't fool around even about small change as the world had learned to its sorrow. They certainly are anything but casual about great voluptuous chunks of money. Oh yes, they would be hunting for her.

She suddenly felt a great longing to be inside the Embassy—and the sooner the better. She moved out to the curb and watched the four lanes of traffic surging toward town. Across the center median another four lanes led toward *Chapultepec* and beyond.

It was almost impossible to squeeze aboard a bus. They were crammed to the doorstep with passengers, but she would find a *pesero*. The *peso* cabs range up and down *Reforma* throughout the day, carrying as many passengers as possible, each for one peso. She watched for the taxi driver with his left arm out the window, holding up his index finger to indicate the one *peso* price.

An old Indian woman with nimble feet and an armful of *serapes* beat her to the last empty seat in one *pesero,* but she and a sleek sideburned boy snagged two empty seats in the next one.

Maura sat close to the window as the cab rocketed up *Reforma,* almost sideswiping a limousine in one abrupt lane change, nearly running down a dignified elderly Dodge in another, but always miraculously missing disaster by a whisker. She sat up straight when she saw the massive Diana Cinema across the street. They were getting close. Then, tall and stately, the Angel came in full view. The tall cylindrical marble monument capped by the golden figure of a winged woman is perhaps the loveliest of all the monuments on *Reforma*. On ahead to the left Maura could see the grand *Maria Isabel,* the most luxurious hotel in Mexico. Just beyond it is the Embassy.

"Aqui, por favor," she said abruptly. As she stumbled over her fellow passengers' feet and handed her *peso* to the driver, she wondered again if she was overdoing the bit. After all, she could get out just across the street from the Embassy. But she had made her choice. The *pesero* scooted off up the boulevard and Maura walked on up the sidewalk. Not far now, she thought.

She walked past towering glass-fronted skyscrapers interspersed with fine shops. Running back several blocks to her right was the most exclusive shopping and dining area in the District. And then she was across the wide boulevard from the Embassy, a substantial square building that rests on concrete arches, all enclosed within a tall fence.

She was waiting at the corner for the light to change when she saw Luis. He waited in the shadow of a tall tree not far from the gates to the Embassy. Of course, there was a back entrance, but there she would have to explain herself. It would take time. The guard would tell her to go in the front way. And all the while she would be out in the open.

And she doubted that Luis was alone. If he was watching the front entrance to the Embassy, he must have a definite plan in mind. He would not stand there to nod good morning.

She turned and walked briskly on up the street, staying to the far right of the wide sidewalk with shoppers and businessmen and tourists as a shield between her and Luis across the street.

She hesitated once. After all, he couldn't plan to shoot her down in the street. All she had to do was gain the gates and she would be safe. But if he spotted her before she reached the gates . . . .

Her pace quickened. It didn't take long to cover the six blocks to the modern 15-story Continental Hilton. She turned into the lobby and hurried toward the phone booths.

She knew the number well. How many times had she called the Embassy? So many times, for so many reasons. During the years her family had lived in Mexico City, she had often called to talk with her father. And since then, after returning to the District as a college student, she had called to chat with old friends, to accept invitations, to inquire about ceremonies, but never with a tale of intrigue.

And it would be the first time she had ever asked to be connected with the Protection Officer, the Embassy official who deals with Americans needing help in Mexico. She wondered idly as she waited for the connection to be made who would be on duty. Would it be Jeff Sisson or perhaps Ron . . . .

And then, crisp and high, a voice she knew only too well came on the line. "Protection Officer. Hadley Morrison speaking."

Maura just stood there. Hadley Morrison. Of all people in the Embassy why did it have to be Hadley Morrison!

"Hello. Hello." Hadley's voice sharpened with each query. "Who's there?"

"Hadley, this is Maura Kelly." And she hesitated.

"Maura," he said blankly. And then, a little upbeat of hope in his voice, "Are you in trouble, dear? Been playing tricks in the Presidential Palace?"

"I haven't played tricks anywhere in years," she replied quickly. Too quickly, of course.

"But we all know your little penchant for jokes, dear," he said. "At least, you explained it at the time as evidence of your youthful high spirits."

She stood there and tightened her suddenly sweaty palm around the receiver. He hadn't forgotten. And he would never forgive. She could see his face as clearly in her mind as she had that day six years ago in the Embassy. She had been working during the summer as an oddjobber, carrying coffee, running errands, a nice job to keep her busy. And she had learned that it was Hadley's birthday. His twenty-seventh. And she had thought up a marvelous joke. She wouldn't do something like that now but the very young can be callous and unwittingly cruel. She had rushed out to a fine men's shop, bought a rather expensive white shirt with french cuffs, and had it giftwrapped. But first she had lovingly and very completely stuffed it with newspapers until it pouched outward like a pouter pigeon. She began to regret her joke when the delivery boy reached Hadley's desk. His thick pudgy neck flushed with pleasure when he

RENDEZVOUS IN VERACRUZ

saw the gaily wrapped package. And he had looked quizzically about at the secretaries and fellow workers as he opened the card and read it out loud. 'To Hadley. Some things are just made for certain people and we knew this must be for you. Love, The Gang.'

She flinched away from remembering his face when he had opened the package.

And then his voice whipped her back to the present and to the telephone, her tenuous link with safety.

"Well, Maura, what do you want? I don't suppose you called up for old time's sake."

"Hadley," she implored, her voice soft and urgent, "please forget and forgive. I haven't called up with a joke. I'm in trouble and I need help and the man I'm running from is keeping a watch on the Embassy."

"What are you talking about?" he asked distantly.

"Hadley, please! Listen to me." She described the message hidden under the clock and her suspicion of Luis and the trap she had set. And she told him about the $100,000 and the cryptic note. And when she finished, there was no response for a long moment.

And then a forced laugh boomed across the wire. "Things must be a bit slow out at school, Maura. And I must say you've shown some ingenuity. I'll have to give you good marks for trying."

"Hadley, you must believe . . . ."

The laughter stopped as suddenly as it had begun and his voice, cold and angry with the anger of years, bit back. "You had me once, Maura. But you'll never do it twice," and the phone slammed into its cradle.

Maura stood there, listening to the empty line, and a quick crackle of fear threaded through her mind.

Slowly, wearily, she hung up the receiver. Grimly, she dialed the Embassy again and she asked to be connected with the Ambassador, explaining who she was and that it was a matter of importance.

The distant voice was kind but firm. "I'm very sorry, Miss Kelly. The Ambassador is in Guadalajara attending an industrial conference and will not return to the District until the end of the week. If it is a serious matter, I can connect you with the Protection Officer."

"Thank you," Maura said dully. "Thank you, but that won't be necessary."

She replaced the receiver and stared blankly at the wall. What was she going to do? What in sweet heaven was she going to do?

The Mexican police? For a moment, she revived. Of course. She would find police headquarters . . . . Her plan lay down and died. And the policeman would call the Protection Officer at the Embassy.

Maura gently rubbed the telephone receiver. Okay. The police were out. The Embassy was out. But she must do something. She couldn't just skip back to *Señora* Alvarez' house and pretend it had never happened—not with $100,000 and a cryptic note in her pocket.

She glanced down at her watch. Eleven-fifteen. At ten this morning she had sent a note to Lin, asking her to stand by the phone in the Journalism office at eleven o'clock.

Maura hesitated for a moment and then she dialed. And she offered up a little prayer that Lin was still there, waiting for her to call.

6
ENCOUNTER AT THE PAWNSHOP

Lin had turned to go a half dozen times, but each time her glance caught and locked on the black telephone sitting on the copy table. Each time she shrugged and turned back to gaze out over the ravine which fell away beneath the balcony of the Journalism Building.

When the phone did ring at fifteen past eleven she swung around, but one of the reporters had already answered. Then the slight blond girl grinned and thrust out the receiver, "It's your call."

"Thank you," Lin said and she took the phone.

"Maura?" she asked immediately.

"Yes. Oh Lin, I'm so glad you waited for me. Listen, I'm really in a jam now. The Embassy won't pay any attention to me—oh, it's a long story, but the fellow who should help thinks I'm the world's biggest practical joker and Ambassador is out of town." She paused, then said quickly, "Look, I don't really think there's any danger to you, but if you don't want to do it, just say so."

"Do what? Maura, what are you talking about? Of course I'll help, but what's going on?"

"I don't want to involve you. Look, the safest thing is for you to know nothing. If anyone asks, you haven't seen me since breakfast. Have you got that? Not since breakfast."

"Okay, okay, I've got that, but what do you want me to do and what's the problem."

"Just do what I ask, please. Go back to the house. Get my passport out of the pink pig. I have an envelope of *pesos* tucked back in my hose drawer. Bring that, too. Put the stuff in a paper bag and be at the National Pawnshop by twelve-thirty. In any case, be sure you make it before two, 'cause it closes then until five."

"All right. I'll hurry. I'll make it," Lin said quickly.

"And Lin, please make sure that no one follows you."

"Maura you must tell . . . ." Lin slowly put the receiver down. Maura had hung up.

She stood there for a moment and felt very isolated from the quiet chatter in the office, the erratic click of typewriters, the everyday humdrum noises.

The blond girl looked up from a stack of copy paper, and said, "Is anything wrong? I didn't mean to eavesdrop, but do you need help?"

Startled, Lin managed at faint smile. "Oh, no thanks. Everything is all right."

She looked down at her watch. She would have to hustle. The next school bus left in about four minutes.

"Oh golly, I've got to run. Listen, thanks a lot for letting me use your phone. It really was an important call."

She grabbed up her notebook and English lit text, slung her shoulder bag over her arm and ran.

As she hurried up the steep stone steps and skirted the end of the Administration Building, the whole conversation with Maura seemed curiously unreal. The campus was as tranquil and beautiful as always. Couples walked hand in hand. Several coeds sat quietly reading on the benches around the base of a vine-covered tree. Nothing was different, but everything was different.

Putting on a burst of speed, Lin reached the bus just

as the driver was ready to go. With an easy smile, he opened the door and she clambered aboard.

"*Gracias, señor, muchas gracias.*"

"*Por nada, señorita.*"

And then she was in her seat and almost without volition she pulled out of her raincoat pocket the note which Della had delivered that morning.

Once again, she read it. "Lin, I've landed in a jam and, like a good girl should, I'm going to hotfoot it to the Embassy. Our note hiding pal is apparently hooked up in something rather big league. I imagine the Embassy will want to talk to you, too, so please hover by the phone in the J office around 11 o'clock. I'll call then. And, if anybody asks, like Luis, for instance, you haven't seen me since breakfast. M."

The note had worried her, Lin thought, but the telephone call was frightening. In the note Maura in her own fashion was serious but lighthearted. On the telephone her voice was strained and tight. And Lin knew that of all her friends it would take a lot to frighten Maura.

Lin closed her eyes briefly, then very efficiently shredded the note into tiny pieces. Pushing up her window, she watched the shreds flutter out onto the highway.

She leaned forward, willing the bus to go faster, although busses in the District never crept. In fact, all cars and busses sped along with more élan than skill, each driver seemingly intent upon proving he was really a veteran of LeMans.

The bus whipped along the curved asphalt road into town and then up the broad tree-lined *Reforma*. Lin got off at *Prado Norte*. She walked swiftly but it seemed as if she moved in quicksand. Finally she reached the house. It gleamed in the sunlight, three stories of white stucco topped with red tile. She pushed through the wrought iron gate, never locked in the daytime, and climbed the rock steps to the front door. The house was swathed in quiet. Next door the maid hummed as she swept the flagstoned path that ran beside the wall that separated the two properties, but from *Señora* Alvarez' house came no sound at all.

Lin stepped into the parquet-floored entry hall and listened. She could faintly hear the soft chatter of the maids in the kitchen, but the swinging door was shut. No one moved or spoke in the common room or dining room.

Lin clattered up the stairs and turned up the hall toward her room. She pushed the door wide and looked about, almost hoping that Maura would be there to say everything was really all right. But their room lay empty and quiet, too.

Lin crossed to the wardrobe and was reaching toward the back for a shopping bag, when her hand paused midway. Her blue capezios were half off the shoe rack. The top of her overnight bag was unlatched. Slowly she straightened and turned to survey the room.

Odds and ends told the story—the desk blotter awry, Maura's jewel case open, the books jumbled in their shelves.

Dimly she heard the crack of the front door closing. Lin whirled about and raced into the hall. The foyer was empty. Someone had just left the house. Could it have been the searcher? Had she surprised someone, her quick steps on the stone entryway warning enough to scare the searcher away?

Lin flew down the stairs and flung open the front door. She looked toward the street. No one. She heard the click of a shoe on stone and turned toward her right. Hurrying up the steps to the apartment atop the servants' quarters was Natalie Mallory. Lin watched as she disappeared inside.

Natalie. Could it have been Natalie? Lin stood there,

disbelief struggling with the facts. Someone had searched the room. And Natalie must have been upstairs—but, of course, she could have been in the kitchen. Perhaps that was it.

Lin turned and hurried to the swinging door. Pushing it open, she poked her head inside and asked Maria, "Have you seen *Señora* Mallory?"

The girl shook her head. "No, *señorita*. She has not been here this morning."

"Thank you," Lin said slowly.

But Natalie had been in the house and she hadn't been downstairs and she had no reason to be upstairs in someone's room. A little picture grew in Lin's mind and cold seeped through her. Natalie pawing through their things. Her own loud steps rat-tatting up the walk. Natalie looking out and quickly, hurriedly darting into one of the other girls' rooms until the coast was clear.

Lin turned again, her face flushed, and started to the front door, the apartment her goal, and then she hesitated. If Natalie really was involved with Luis in some fashion, she would deny everything. And it would be her word against Lin's.

And time was wasting. She must meet Maura. She would do something about Natalie when she got back.

Once upstairs again, it didn't take long to gather up the things. She dropped the passport and the envelope with money into the bag. Then she pulled out the envelope. Opening it, she counted 600 *pesos*. Maura probably wouldn't need much more, whatever she planned, but, just in case, Lin peeled another 240 *pesos* out of her own billfold and stuffed them in the envelope. Then she added a comb, toothbrush, toothpaste, a slender box of *Entero-Vioformo* tablets, and a nightgown. She sighed and shook her head. It all seemed mad, to be packing a paper bag as if for a fugitive—but Maura had sounded frightened.

Grimly, she once again hurried back up *Prado Norte*

Encounter at the Pawnshop 67

to *Reforma*. She hailed a *pesero* and sat back in the corner, oblivious alike to the sagging upholstery and the cab's rackety progress. Soon, she would know what was happening—and what had happened to frighten Maura. In only a little while she would be at the Pawnshop and she would discover what Maura was running from, then she would know how to help.

She paid no attention to their progress up *Reforma* or to the traffic. She didn't look back at all. She didn't see the red VW that hung so skillfully behind the cab.

The *pesero* was turning from *Reforma* onto *Juarez* when Lin remembered Maura's plea to make sure she wasn't followed. As the cab neared the dignified *Del Prado,* a favorite hotel of wealthy Americans, Lin called out, *"Aqui, por favor."*

Jumping out, she thought with satisfaction that if a car had followed, she would soon be lost to sight in the milling surge of pedestrians.

She hurried on up the street, not even sparing a glance for the beautiful central park, the *Alameda,* across the street. She passed so many of the famous landmarks of the city, the *Alameda,* the Palace of Fine Arts, the gleaming new *Latino-Americano* Building, the tallest building in Latin America.

As she made her way through the thick crowds on narrow sidewalks, the VW pulled into the curb and Tommy Mallory jumped out. And as he moved hurriedly forward, he pulled the brim of his cap low on his forehead and turned up the collar of his blue trenchcoat.

The swirling noonday press of people only increased as she neared the *Zócalo,* the District's main plaza and the center of Mexico's government. The crowd was a fascinating mixture of the primitive and the sophisticated. Street vendors made their way with baskets of their wares, hot foods, *serapes,* sandals, selling so much for so little. Conservatively dressed Mexican businessmen in sleek immaculate black suits and brilliantly black shoes walked slowly, never hurried. Barefoot men in ragged khaki pants and shirts hawked lottery tickets. A mink-coated American dowager limped a little but marched determinedly on, her guidebook at the ready.

Lin looked down at her watch and increased her pace. Twelve-fifteen. She clutched the brown paper shopping bag and dodged her way on up the street, past chattering groups of salesgirls on their lunch break, past Indian families walking slowly with eyes wide at the bustling city, past ragged groups of boys lounging aimlessly on street corners.

When she reached the *Zócalo,* she turned to her left and walked under the Arcades where dozens of small shops offered silver and leather and straw work to the tourists.

She crossed *Cinco de Mayo* and the *Nacional Monte de Piedad* loomed before her. She hesitated momentarily on the sidewalk, wondering where in the huge old building that Maura intended for her to go. She stepped inside the stone corridor and looked around.

She had visited the Pawnshop once before. A national institution, it had been opened in 1775 by a wealthy mine owner as a place where people of all classes could pawn valuables to borrow money and later redeem their goods at no interest. Now the government ran it, charging a small interest rate. Unredeemed articles are sold at regular auction and thousands of articles are sold daily.

The *Monte de Piedad* has everything—books, jewelry, typewriters, harps, antiques, bicycles, paintings, records. Silver and gold and jade, porcelain and plastic and leather, it is all here, so many tributes to necessity in so many forms.

Lin looked uncertainly down the corridor. To her left was a row of rooms with different types of goods. Down a bit, double doors opened to the right into a huge room where an auction was now underway.

On the sidewalk, a young man in a blue trenchcoat paused, as if he too were uncertain where to turn next.

Lin waited a moment more then walked toward the first room to her left. Surely Maura would look in each room until she found Lin.

The brown-haired girl turned decisively into the narrow doorway with gold lettering announcing, *Antiguedades, Pinturas, Candiles, Cristal.* She looked down the narrow length, crowded beyond description with baroque chests, model galleons, gilt-framed paintings, cut glass vases, marble-topped teak tables, chandeliers, and more.

Lin stepped around an immense carved oak sideboard. Maura wasn't here. She leaned close to a picture of a rather lopsided whaling ship teetering on the brink of a mammoth wave and tried to decide whether to stay here or move on to another room. She turned over the price tag.

She paid little attention when someone, his back to her, squeezed past her down the narrow aisle, murmuring, *"Perdón, por favor."*

Lin glanced quickly about when footsteps sounded near, but it was only a boy. She looked at a set of sterling candelabras and was reaching for the price tag when she felt a hesitant tug on her sleeve and looked down into the dark bright eyes of the raggedly dressed but handsome little boy whose footsteps she had heard.

"Señorita Prescott?" he whispered.

"Yes," she replied as softly.

"I come from your friend, *Señorita* Kelly." He spoke so softly and so quickly in his liquid Spanish that Lin understood only Maura's name. She bent closer to him, but he moved a pace away and pointed to the intricately rigged model of a galleon. "Please, *señorita,* look at this, not at me. Your friend said someone may be watching you."

The words chilled Lin, but she understood well enough. The boy had come for Maura because she didn't dare come for herself.

Lin moved closer to the ship and lightly touched a stiff white sail. Pretending to ignore the boy, she whispered in halting Spanish, "You have come from *Señorita* Kelly?"

"Yes," he replied. "Her package. Give it to me and I will deliver it to her."

Lin started to turn toward him, but he hissed, "No, no. Put it on the floor, then walk away."

The girl took a deep breath, then bent close to a slender-necked copper teapot. She tried to put the sack down unobtrusively. As she straightened and turned away, she stepped into the aisle.

A few feet past Lin, Tommy Mallory looked swiftly around and realized with a surge of panic that he was trapped. There was no exit other than the door through which he had entered—and Lin stood between him and the quickly retreating boy.

Indecision kept him motionless for a moment, but, as the boy reached the door, Tommy swore under his breath and hurried up the narrow aisle.

"Lin, hey, Lin," he called out. "Hey, somebody's stolen your bag. Good thing I saw it. Let me by and I'll grab him."

The girl whirled to face him, her eyes blank and then, slowly, suspicion flooded them.

"Tommy, what are you doing here?"

He tried to edge past her but there was no room.

"Lin, that boy grabbed your sack. Let me go after him. Hurry."

She didn't move. "You've made a mistake," she said coolly. "I don't have a sack."

His blue eyes flickered with anger. "But you had . . . ." And then his voice trailed off and his eyes fell away from hers. How could he say she had carried a sack when she left the house? That would reveal that he had followed her. And he couldn't admit that.

Uncertain what to do, he stood there for another moment and then realized that the boy was gone. While he had tried to get past Lin, the boy had gone—and he must have gone to Maura!

Angry and frustrated, Tommy grabbed Lin's arm. "Let me by. Now, I tell you."

She shrugged and slowly stepped out of his way. She watched his quick and almost violent progress with a hint of sadness. First, Natalie in their room, and now Tommy, who must have followed her to the Pawnshop. Her friends. At least, she had thought them her friends. She had liked them. She was startled to feel the quick prick of tears behind her eyes. Then she too was moving angrily up the aisle and out the door. She half ran to the sundrenched sidewalk and shaded her eyes.

Had she delayed Tommy long enough? Surely she had. Because if he had found the boy. . . . She looked across the mammoth paved *Zócalo* and nowhere did she see Tommy. Her gaze swung back. Across the street rose the imposing Cathedral which dominates the square. In the courtyard vendors moved about, offering sacred medals, rosaries, candies and balloons to tourists and to devout families coming with children to be baptized.

Her searching gaze followed the high iron fence that surrounds the church and her shoulders slumped in relief. Tommy stood on the sidewalk beside the church, scanning the *Zócalo* and the sidewalks. Finally, he shook his head and walked to the red VW parked at the curb. He bent near the window and in an instant raised up to wave his arm hopelessly in the direction of the plaza. Lin saw Natalie in the driver's seat. She, too, shrugged. Tommy climbed in and the VW started up.

Lin looked after it with a sense of satisfaction. So

Tommy hadn't found the boy—and he wouldn't find Maura. Then her feeling of well-being seeped away. Tommy and Natalie hadn't found Maura, but then neither had she. And Maura needed help.

The girl looked again at the immense vista of the *Zócalo*. The huge barren paved plaza was dotted here and there with people crossing, an Indian alone in simple white cotton shirt and pants, a family group, American tourists, schoolgirls on an outing, but no one who looked like Maura or the boy she had sent.

Lin sighed and wearily began to walk back toward *Madero*. There were people everywhere, but nowhere could she see Maura.

7
A RICH AMERICANA

In a narrow side street north of the *Zócalo* little shops tumbled their wares over onto the sidewalk. Makeshift awnings provided shade for both hawkers and customers. A few tourists shopped for bargains, haggling with little success in their inadequate Spanish. Mexican shoppers smiled and easily and surely beat down the prices.

The black scarf still wound tightly around her hair, Maura stood deep in the dingy interior of a leatherwork shop. She kept a wary eye on the doorway as she played the expected charade with the shopkeeper. She picked up a pair of *huaraches,* the leather sandals so common in the Mexican countryside, and held them in the light for a critical inspection.

The small tradesman could detect an *Americana* even in a shapeless raincoat.

"Ah," he protested. "the *señorita* doesn't want these shoes," and grabbed them from her.

Maura grabbed them right back. In her quick and fluent Spanish she explained she was buying them for her maid. *"Cuál es el precio?"*

"Cincuenta pesos, señorita," and he launched into an impassioned description of their excellent workmanship.

She interrupted with a curt shake of her head and

volubly discussed their patent inferiority, concluding with an offer of 15 *pesos.*

The owner was stricken. He protested. He took back the *huaraches* with a saddened air.

The deal was finally made at 25 *pesos,* two dollars in U.S. currency.

As she paid for the sandals and waited for them to be wrapped in old newspaper and tightly tied with twine, she moved a little nearer the doorway and peered anxiously down the street.

The shopkeeper's immediate recognition of her as an American brought a prickly awareness of how easily she could be spotted unless she shed her conspicuously *norte* clothes.

But she couldn't manage the plan which had slowly taken shape in her mind unless José returned.

She scanned the crowded sidewalk. She was gambling her safety on the honesty of a street urchin, but she had seen no other choice.

Turning back into the store, she accepted her parcel with a smile. And then she stood by a pile of intricately tooled billfolds, fingering first one and then another. It was cool in the shop, the thick old walls holding the chill of night, but she could feel a light film of sweat on her face.

If José didn't come . . . and then she felt a shy tug on her sleeve and she looked down at him. He had slipped into the store as swiftly and lightly as a shadow.

"Aquí, señorita." And he handed the precious paper sack to her.

She closed her eyes briefly in relief. He had come. She reached into her purse, pulled out a 20 *peso* bill and tucked it into his hand.

"Thank you, José."

He looked at it, startled. "You only promised me five *pesos, señorita."*

"I am grateful, José."

His eyes gleamed. Twenty *pesos*. It was only $1.60 to Maura. It was more money than José had ever held in his hand.

"Muchisimas gracias," he said with dignity. Pocketing the note very carefully in his ragged shorts, he turned and slipped out the doorway to disappear in an instant.

Maura looked after him regretfully. She hated to see him go. It was very lonely to be a fugitive, but it was up to her from this point on. José couldn't help her now.

She waited until the crowd was thick before stepping out onto the sidewalk. She moved from one shop to another, mentally ticking off her purchases from the list in her mind, a shapeless black cotton dress, two black *rebozos,* a woven basket, a packet of needles and a spool of black thread.

As she left the little street of shops, she walked eastward, turning onto a street of rundown tenements. Many remnants of original and beautiful Colonial architecture still stood in this dusty and poverty-begrimed area. She walked with her paper sack held high, shielding her face as much as possible. Two blocks later she turned south down an old, old street narrow enough to almost be an alleyway. It lay deserted in the noon quiet. With a quick look around, she slipped into the doorway of a tenement and opened wide the basket she had bought. Into it she plumped the paper sack from Lin, her purchases and the contents of her purse. Then she stuffed the American handbag into a refuse box. It would be a prize for someone.

When she reached *Madero,* she was four blocks from her goal, the old Sanborn's where she had first met Luis. Just a sentimental journey, she thought wryly.

When she saw the bright blue tiles that gave Sanborn's its title, House of Tiles, she hesitated for a moment, standing still on the sidewalk while people surged past.

If there was any one place in the District that you could count on finding Americans, it was Sanborn's. And it just wasn't the day to bump into friends—or enemies. But it was the closest spot for what she needed and so she slipped in the front door, whipped past the candy section and turned into the drugstore department where the shelves and counters were full of the lotions and cosmetics popular in the States. Her purchase made, she quickly regained the sidewalk.

Glancing up and down *Madero*, she swiftly crossed, her destination a modest but good hotel, the *Guardiola*. She darted through the little curio shop in the narrow entranceway, then paused at the main door to effect a startling transformation. Pulling off the black scarf, she flung back her head and her thick mane of red hair swung free, flambouyant and arresting. She pushed open the door and moved across the lobby with the casual grace and self-confidence of a wealthy American. She easily dominated the small lobby—and the desk clerk.

"I do hope you've a vacancy," she said charmingly. "We don't have reservations because we hadn't planned to stop over in the District until we were on the way back from Yucatán, but the car seems to have something wrong with it. My husband is at the garage now. I'd like a double with a bath, please."

And so, with her calm assumption of welcome and her distinctive air of American affluence, Maura managed to engage a room in a respectable hotel, something that would be very difficult for a lone young Mexican woman to do.

She signed the register, Mr. and Mrs. Norman Wilson. The bellboy showed her to her room and she tipped him five *pesos*.

Once alone, she locked the door then leaned against it and smiled, even if a little wearily. The deskman had taken her at her valuation, all right. This was obviously one of the best rooms in the hotel. The door opened into a tiled hall. To the right was the bathroom. To the left the bedroom, complete with two double beds, a dressing table, a bureau, three chairs—and huge casement windows overlooking *Madero*.

She crossed to the windows. Across the street was the House of Tiles. She looked up and down the street and, as she did so, realized that she was instinctively checking for pursuers. She moved abruptly back from the window. There was no reason at all for anyone to find her here, but she had better get busy. She couldn't afford to stay too long in the hotel, because soon enough the deskman would begin to wonder where Mr. Wilson was and their luggage.

She took her little sack from Sanborn's into the bathroom, slipped out of her skirt and blouse, and set to work. It didn't take long. She rinsed the last of the stain from the lavatory, then straightened and looked long in the mirror.

A stranger stared back at her. The thick black hair, still damp from the rinse, emphasized her dark eyes and fair skin. She felt shockingly unreal as she stared at the mirrored face, but she also felt much safer.

Carefully, thoroughly, she scrubbed out the lavatory until no trace of the rinse remained. When she finished, she picked up the empty container and its box and dropped them into the wastebasket. She turned to go out, then turned back and, with a smile that held little amusement, bent down and fished them out again. She might get the hang of this fugitive business yet.

Once back in the bedroom, she dropped the revealing trash into the bottom of her basket. She rolled up her skirt and sweater and blouse and pressed them deep inside the basket, then dropped her shoes on top.

The shapeless black dress lay waiting on the near bed. She pulled it on and whirled to look in the mirror. Its high neck and long sleeves made her look older. In another moment, she had the *huaraches* on and one of the black *rebozos* around her shoulders.

She looked carefully around the room. All that remained of Maura Kelly was the pink envelope with her *pesos,* her blue-backed passport and her billfold. She dropped these into the basket then covered them with the other black *rebozo,* tucking it neatly until nothing beneath showed.

She nodded her head in satisfaction. She was ready to go. She looked down at her watch and a queer breathlessness caught at her chest. How many plainly dressed Mexican women wore a delicate-faced Swiss watch on a white gold band?

She unsnapped the band and pushed the watch far down in her basket. Many mistakes like that and she'd never reach her destination.

It was almost three o'clock. It was time and time past to get free of the hotel. She felt pressed now, anxious to be gone. Quickly, she pulled out a page of hotel stationery, wrote *"Para la cuenta,"* and put it on top of the dresser. She hurried out to the little hallway and checked the rate board that each Mexican hotel is required by law to post. For this room, the charge was 105 *pesos* a night. Maura went back to the dresser, pulled out her envelope and peeled off two fifty-peso bills and a five, then left another twenty in a separate pile for the maid. She left the key, too.

When the door clicked shut behind her, she wished for a moment that she hadn't left the key, that she could return to the room yet a while longer. But she knew that the sense of security was illusory. She wouldn't be safe until she was far from here, far from the District.

She stood for a moment, listening and looking. The upper floors of the *Guardiola* were built around a huge skylight. She looked over the small railing that guarded the area and could see down to the second floor. It was quiet and silent everywhere.

Encouraged, she walked toward the back of the hotel and the service stairs. She made it down the dark and narrow stairs to the first floor, then hung back in the shadow as a chambermaid slowly emptied a hamper of soiled sheets. When she stepped into a small storeroom, Maura moved quietly past and out the back door. Once in the alleyway behind the hotel she walked at a sedate pace, a maid going home, until she reached a busy cross street and merged into the crowds. With her jet black hair, pale face and shapeless dress, she was undistinguished and indistinguishable.

8
NO PLACE FOR
A NICE GIRL

Lin sat in the common room, her ancient history text in her lap, her head bent as if she were reading. Occasionally she would turn a page to bolster the illusion, but her attention was divided between the hall where the telephone rested on a small square redwood table and the common room where Natalie Mallory sat gracefully in the black wingback chair by the fireplace.

It seemed a lifetime ago that she had hurried to the National Pawnshop, worried but at the same time confident that when she saw Maura everything would be explained. She looked down at her watch. Four-thirty. The afternoon had dragged interminably on as she and Natalie shared the common room.

What was Natalie waiting for? For Maura to come home? For Maura to call Lin? Natalie had never, to Lin's knowledge, spent an entire afternoon in the common room. She could only be here because of Maura.

Lin almost slammed her book shut a dozen times, ready to ask straight out. Then her throat would close on the question. How could she possibly accuse Natalie of searching their room? How could she possibly accuse Tommy of following her in hopes of finding Maura? It all sounded mad, absurd.

The telephone rang and both Lin and Natalie swung

around to look at it. And both sank back into their chairs when Tina padded past the common room to call the *señora* to the phone.

Lin sighed then and did shut her book. She couldn't sit here while the day dwindled away and just wait on the fading hope that Maura would call. If Maura had intended to call, she had had plenty of time to do it. So Maura wasn't going to call—and that left Lin holding a very fat bag.

Restlessly Lin pushed up from the stiff wicker chair and walked to the windows. Lengthening shadows muted the glow of the rust red carnations that bordered the flagstoned walk to the gate. It was late afternoon now. Soon it would be dinnertime and Lin must decide before then what she would tell *Señora* Alvarez.

If she didn't cover for Maura, if she didn't spin some sort of story, the fuse would be lit and heaven knew how far the bang would be heard. First, *Señora* Alvarez would immediately contact the University. And, since Maura had an excellent record and had never been involved in any sort of dubious scrape, the University would take her absence very seriously indeed. This would mean prompt notification of the police and probably the Embassy.

Lin frowned and rubbed her hand against the cool plastered wall. Maura had tried to go to the Embassy, but they hadn't believed her. And if the Embassy wouldn't believe her, why should the police? But where had she gone and what was she going to do?

The girl turned, oblivious to Natalie's watchful gaze, and paced back toward the hall, immersed in her problem.

Okay, she decided, Maura was in trouble, but she couldn't go to the Embassy or the police. Therefore, she would certainly be horrified if the University set them on her trail.

Lin reached the wicker chair and slumped down into

it. She didn't see any choice, really. She had to cover for Maura.

Her opportunity came as everyone settled around the table for dinner, including, Lin saw, the Mallorys. The *señora* bowed her head to say grace then looked sharply at the empty place beside Lin.

"Where is Maura this evening? She didn't tell me she would miss dinner."

"Didn't she call you this morning, *señora?*" Lin asked in apparent surprise.

"No, she didn't," the woman replied, but the edge of worry in her voice faded. "Does she have plans this evening?"

Lin noticed, without seeming to, that both of the Mallorys were listening intently. She smiled widely. "Not only for this evening, the lucky rat. Her folks called her out at school this morning and they are all off to Acapulco for the rest of the week. Maura was so thrilled."

The *señora* nodded her head then and swiftly said grace and the meal began.

As Lin lifted her soup spoon, Natalie said casually, "I didn't see Maura come back to pack."

Lin swallowed the soup which tasted like nothing at all, but she met Natalie's gaze steadily. "She didn't bother. You know they have a beach home there. I guess she'll have everything she needs."

Natalie stared at her for a long moment and almost spoke again, but stopped at Tommy's slight headshake.

Lin finished her soup and ate steadily through the roast pork without tasting a bite of it.

If there had been any doubt in her mind, it was gone now. The Mallorys were involved, all right. She laid down her fork and then as quickly picked it up again. To mask her worry, she turned to Della and began a spirited discussion of library rules and procedures.

". . . and I just don't see why you can't recheck a book

for the full time. I mean, sometimes you can't finish . . . ."

Somehow or other, the dinner came to an end, but afterward Lin could never remember what she had eaten. She begged off a bridge game on the plea that she must work on a term paper, but once upstairs she left the door open in case the phone rang. Then she sat at her desk, aimlessly doodling squares and boxes and squiggles.

And she tried to decide what she was going to do. She must do something. She had covered for Maura for the time being, but the lie couldn't fly forever. It was such a thin little lie. What if the phone rang in a moment and it was Maura's mother? Her mother did phone every so often, just to chat.

Lin tossed down her pencil and ran a hand through her thick tawny hair. If she just had someone to confide in. But she didn't. None of the other girls were in any position to make a better judgment than she was. And, if she told the *señora,* the hounds would be in full cry.

Lin sighed and pushed back her chair. She walked up and down the room, back and forth. Finally she stopped at the broad front window. The shutters still stood wide and the chill night air flowed in. She put her palms on the broad flat sill and leaned out. Street lamps glistened dimly. Lighted windows dotted the houses up and down the street. In the stillness, she heard the slow even footsteps of the *velador,* the nightwatchman making his rounds.

She shivered and pulled the shutters shut. Suddenly, she wished she was back home in Missouri where residents didn't have to band together to hire a nightwatchman to protect them as they slept. And then she felt ashamed. How unfair she was. Mexico certainly didn't have any corner on thievery and vandalism.

Her wish to be home was easy to understand, of course. At home, she would know whom to turn to, what to do.

Here, in a foreign country, she felt isolated and terribly alone.

And she wasn't, she realized, facing up to the problem. Pacing and fuming and wishing weren't helping her make a decision.

She sat down at her desk and cupped her chin in her hands. What was she going to do? Suddenly, it seemed simple. She would continue as she had begun, trying to help Maura. And how best could she do that?

The girl picked up a pencil and began to chew on it. Obviously Maura had caught Luis out in some scheme that was both illegal and dangerous. Not so obviously, the scheme must involve both of the Mallorys. And the only possible way Lin could get any idea of what was going on would be to watch the Mallorys.

She pushed back her chair and walked decisively to the wardrobe. Her jacket was in her hands when she heard faintly the ring of the telephone. She dropped the coat and ran out of the room.

She was halfway down the stairs when she heard Tina say, "*Señorita* Prescott? *Sí, ella está aquí.*"

Lin finished the stairs in a rush and scooped up the receiver.

When the deep masculine voice spoke, her shoulders slumped for a moment and then she recognized the voice and stood very straight.

"Lin, this is Luis. I must talk to you about Maura."

The girl stood silent. She gripped the receiver so tightly her hand ached.

"What do you mean?" she demanded finally.

"You know what I mean," he said angrily.

"I don't," she objected. "I don't know at all."

"Maura's in trouble, real trouble. I have a message for you to give her."

"But I can't give her a message. I don't know where she is!"

"I don't believe you," he said flatly. He paused, then added, "But that's all right. If you don't want to help her then forget I called. Just . . . ."

"Wait a minute," she said quickly. "If she gets in touch with me, I can give her the message. Tell me what it is."

"Not on the phone," he said shortly. "I'll come by and get you. Be out in front of the house in fifteen minutes." And without waiting for her reply, he hung up.

Slowly she replaced the receiver. So Luis had come out in the open. He sounded angry and dangerous. And what could be the message that he wouldn't give it over the phone? Why didn't he just tell her whatever it was?

She began to walk up the stairs. She didn't want to go out with Luis. She was afraid of him. Once upstairs in her room, she walked to the window and pushed it open. It was dark and still and the scattered lights in the houses and along the street were only small patches of cheer in the dark.

All right, if she didn't want to go with Luis, she wouldn't. She didn't have to go downstairs and wait out in front of the house.

But what if the message really was important? Important to Maura's safety? Her throat felt dry as dust as she pulled her coat from the wardrobe. She couldn't take the chance. She must go.

Outside, she leaned against the wall bordering the sidewalk. She was all alone on the street tonight. No one walked a dog. The *velador* hadn't reached this point on his rounds again. She stood up straight and jammed her hands in her pockets and realized that she was cold, cold not only with the chill of night, but cold with fear. Luis was the center of something dark and frightening.

She almost turned to go back into the house, but then she remembered Maura's strained voice over the telephone that morning and she stayed where she was. If she went with Luis, she might find out what was frightening Maura and the more she knew, the better she would be able to help her roommate.

The MG seemed to fling itself up the street. It squealed to a stop. Luis leaned over from the driver's seat to open the door.

"Get in. Hurry," he commanded.

She climbed into the car and pulled shut the door, and suddenly there was no turning back. As the car rocketed up *Prado Norte* and swung left onto *Reforma,* she watched his grim profile in the splashes of light from the street lamps.

The MG whined as he darted from one lane to another in the heavy evening traffic. They passed the Angel and the Embassy, the Continental Hilton and the biggest Sanborn's and then the car curved to the right onto *Juarez,* the main street which leads finally to the *Zócalo.*

As they passed Alameda Park, Lin started to speak, but when she looked at Luis hunched behind the wheel she said nothing.

The Palace of Fine Arts glittered on their left and ahead she could see the lighted top of the *Latino-Americano* Building. When the light changed, Luis turned left onto *San Juan de Letran* and Lin sat up straighter.

"Where are we going, Luis?" she asked and she realized with dismay that her voice sounded thin.

"A place I know," he said shortly. "Nobody will look for us there."

Finally he veered to the right. It was a section of the city that Lin didn't know. The buildings were old, but not with grace and beauty. The meanness of poverty was reflected in the patched and boarded windows, in the narrowing of the streets.

She said nothing more, but sat still and stiff and as close to the door as she could. The car finally rolled to a stop in a dim side street and she loked uneasily about.

She clutched the door handle when a man lurched out of a nearby doorway and stumbled past, his hand sliding along the rough adobe wall for support.

Luis reached across her and opened the door. And the warnings that had buzzed in her mind throughout the silent but furiously paced drive shrilled into alarm. A Mexican man is bred to courtesy. The mere fact that Luis hadn't alighted to open the door for her indicated much more than bad manners. It spelled danger.

"Luis, where are we?" she asked, and she didn't move.

"A place where we can talk. Come on." And it was a command. At his insistent pressure against her arm, she slid out of the car. On the sidewalk, she shook loose from his grip and pulled her coat close around her.

She could hear the thin ragged sound of trumpets and volleys of laughter and harsh voices raised in argument. Luis took her arm and lead her up the sidestreet and around the corner.

Lin stopped short. They stood at the end of a dimly lighted plaza. Garish neon lights flickered above several night spots. Bands of seedy musicians wandered about, hoping to find someone willing to pay a few *pesos* to hear them play. And men were everywhere, thick on the sidewalks, scattered across the square.

Lin held back. She knew where they were, although she had never been here before. The *Plaza Garibaldi,* the center of sleazy bars and night spots, some of them catering to tourists, most of them not. A place where no nice Mexican woman would come and only foolish Americans.

Luis gripped her elbow tightly and pushed her ahead. She planted her heels on the cobbled sidewalk and resisted.

"Luis, I won't go here."

He turned and bent close to her and, with a little

catch of fear, she realized that he had been drinking—
and not just a little.

"Oh yes you will," he said and his voice and eyes were
ugly.

A sharp hard pain laced up her arm as his grip tightened. "Oh yes you will, because I have to find Maura. I
have to," and he pushed her along the rough sidewalk
toward a narrow doorway with a red light flickering above
it.

Luis led her through an arched doorway and a milling
throng of men, some with glasses tight in hand, some
with wine-filled *bodegas,* made way for them. Dark eyes
followed them hostilely.

Inside it was noise and dust and stench. The sweat of
unwashed men mingled with the thick sweetness of
cheap perfume. Hard-faced women turned to stare at
Lin. The throbbing din ebbed a little as heads turned
to watch their slow progress across the crowded room.
Tables nestled next to tables with barely room enough
for passage between them.

They squeezed behind a little table next to the wall.
Lin sank onto the hard bench, her cheeks flaming. How
dared Luis bring her to a place like this. But even as
she glanced fearfully around, she realized that they
had caused only a ripple of comment. No one, now, was
watching them, and perhaps the hostility she had felt
was only the natural dislike for those who do not belong—
as she and Luis obviously did not belong. She began
to breathe more freely. No one was paying any attention
to them now. Raucous laughter resounded. Bottles
clinked. The bands, two of them, played loudly and dis-
sonantly, a cha cha rhythm mingling oddly with the wail-
ing trumpet of a southern coastal song.

Preremptorily Luis waved down a waitress.

"Dos tequilas, prontamente."

His hand drummed impatiently on the warped table-top. Lin watched his face, the skin tight drawn over the cheekbones, the bunched eyebrows, the thinned lips, and remained silent.

When the liquor came, colorless in squat tumblers, Luis sprinkled salt on the back of his left hand, then took a deep drink from the glass. Lin watched patiently as he completed the ritual, flicking some of the salt from the back of his hand to his tongue, then sucking on a lime picked from those heaped in a small wooden bowl in the center of the table.

He looked dully across the table and pushed her glass closer to her. "Drink up."

"In a minute, Luis, but first, what message do you want me to give Maura if she calls?"

He stared at her for a long moment then upended his glass and greedily swallowed the rest of the *tequila*.

"Don't pretend with me," he said harshly.

"What do you mean?" Lin asked slowly.

"You know what Maura did. She told you."

"No. She told me nothing."

His face flushed a dull ugly red. "She must have told you," he insisted.

She shook her head and made no answer.

"But this morning you came back to the house and then you took a sack and went downtown. We were sure you were going to meet Maura, then that boy came for the sack and Tommy couldn't get past you to follow him. But you must know where Maura was going!"

"I don't know anything, Luis, except that you and the Mallorys are mixed up in something illegal and that Maura is afraid of you."

"But you must know!" he repeated. And then he spoke in a coaxing, reasonable voice as if to a child. "You see, Lin, I have to get it back. Maura took the envelope and I have to get it back." He looked around the room, fear glistening in his eyes. "You see, I had to call the village and send word to *El Jefe* that it was gone. Then his man in the village called back and said *El Jefe* was sending Jaime and Carlos."

Lin bent over the table, trying to make sense of the mumbled hurried words, but all she clearly understood was Luis' fear of *El Jefe*, whoever he might be.

"Who is *El Jefe?*" she asked.

Luis' handsome face quivered. "If I can't find Maura, he won't believe me. He'll think I took the money."

"What money?" she asked sharply.

He stared at her and despair clouded his eyes. "You must know! You have to tell me where she's hiding, that rotten thieving . . . ."

"Luis, what are you talking about?" she demanded. "What did Maura do?"

"What did she do!" he cried shrilly, "She took the money, that's what she did. And they won't believe me. Jaime and Carlos will be looking for me now and when they find me . . . . By the time they know I don't have the money, I'll be dead."

With a shaking hand, he picked up her tumbler of *tequila* and downed it at one gulp.

Lin stared at him. His dark face was sallow and his eyes shifted first one way and then the other.

"Don't look at me like that," he ordered loudly and his hand caught her wrist again. "What was in that sack? Maybe you . . . ."

He stopped abruptly and his nostrils flared wide. He stared out across the room.

Lin looked too but all she saw was the mass of tables, the people everywhere. The table lurched and she turned back to Luis, but he was scrambling unsteadily to his feet. He turned and moved clumsily but swiftly toward the back, shoving his way through the knots of men by the long bar that extended the length of the huge room.

She watched him go, then looked toward the door. She saw two men bulling their way through the crowd and then, in unison, they swerved, changing their course from the table toward the back of the room.

Both men wore khaki pants and short sleeve white shirts. Burned mahogany-brown from the sun, they walked lithely, their arms free and loose—and they moved as hunters move.

Lin sat stiffly on her bench. She could no longer see Luis. And then the men began to hurry and they too were lost to view.

Her heart thudded painfully and her hands clenched the edge of the rough wooden table. She was alone—alone in a cheap nightclub in a tawdry district of a huge foreign city, a city where nice women rarely appeared in even the best of bars.

Would she be able to make her way out unmolested? She would have to cross that floor filled with men who were assured by her mere presence in this place that her character was questionable.

She looked about and saw that the glances had started, the frank appraisals begun. At the long bar that stretched along the wall, she heard a burst of laughter. She half turned and saw a group of men eyeing her. One drunken young man called out something to his friends and in the raucous laughter that followed he began to walk unsteadily toward her.

RENDEZVOUS IN VERACRUZ

9

"WHAT THE HECK, JACK!"

As the film flicked to an end in the modest movie house, Maura stepped into the aisle and moved inconspicuously in the wake of a family group, the father carrying one sleeping child, the mother herding three more before her. On the street Maura merged with the milling crowd at a bus stop.

Once on board the bus, she surreptitiously glanced at her watch in her basket. It was almost nine o'clock, late enough and dark enough for the next step in her plan.

The bus trundled out *Reforma*. When it passed the Embassy, Maura began to watch the streets closely. It was right along here somewhere. Two blocks more and she rose, pulled the cord and struggled up the crowded aisle to the rear. The bus stopped and, as she stepped out, two young Mexicans leaned out a near window and offered to walk with her. Ignoring them, she moved briskly off down the side street.

She walked for three blocks, passing apartments, old homes, a warehouse, an occasional shop. She stopped finally beneath a street lamp and looked around. And then she breathed a sigh of relief. There it was, a four-story apartment house wedged between an old home and a meat market.

She crossed the street and walked slowly up to the

apartment house. The second-floor front apartment was dark. Now, if it just turned out to be empty. It should be, but life was very uncertain, as she had come to appreciate during this long day. Nancy Dickinson had told Maura yesterday that she and Bob were leaving for Cuernavaca after school Tuesday afternoon.

Maura slipped quietly into the foyer and walked up the stairs to the second floor. She stood for a moment outside the Dickinsons' apartment, her ear pressed to the panel. No sound came from within.

Quickly she slipped to the window at the end of the hall, a few feet away, and ran her hand beneath the sill. Her fingers found the small hump of tape. She smiled a little grimly. When Nancy had regaled a group at coffee one day with the saga of the key strewing habits of the Dickinsons' and their eventual decision to always have an extra taped beneath the hall window sill, it had never occurred to Maura that one night she would make use of it.

She tiptoed back to the door and started to put the key in the lock, then hesitated. It would scarcely do to barge in on a sleeping Bob and Nancy. She knocked softly and waited a slow count to ten before she slipped the key into the lock. Once inside, she shut the door and twisted the lock. Flipping on the light switch, she looked quickly around and her tense nerves relaxed. To her left was a wicker divan and two easy chairs. A desk and a day bed, covered with a bright spread, were pushed against the opposite wall. A curtained alcove to her right held the tiny kitchen and the bath was tucked beyond the door beside the alcove. The small apartment was quite empty of Dickinsons.

She slipped out of her *huaraches* and padded to the kitchen. The tin percolator, clean and dry, sat on the two-burner stove. Maura started some coffee, then fixed a sandwich of baloney and rye, wishing the while that Nancy didn't sweep the kitchen quite so clean when leaving for a holiday.

But the sandwich and coffee were marvelously refreshing. She stretched out on the divan with a tufted red pillow at her back and enjoyed every mouthful. She refilled her coffee cup and sipped it, but the sense of ease slowly faded. She had much to do yet tonight.

Briskly Maura rose and carried her plate and cup to the tiny kitchen. She washed and dried them and returned to the living room, but this time she sat at the desk.

She must decide definitely where to go and how to get there. A close friend of her father's headed the American Consulate in Guadalajara and her father's cousin Benjamin was second in command at the American Consulate in Veracruz.

Maura frowned and drew out of the basket the envelope which she had removed from beneath the clock. The money she piled neatly on the desk. She reread the message: 20° 42′ N, 96° 15′ W, 2400 hours, 25 October. Password—Do you like fish? The answer will be—Yes, especially the fish of the hills.

The girl pushed back her chair and kneeled before the homemade bookcases that sat beside the desk. She smiled and reached for the *Goode's World Atlas*. Flipping to a map of Mexico, she traced the lines. Her eyes narrowed. Now she had a pinpoint on the map and a very enlightening one.

She sat back on her heels and the picture slipped into sharper focus. The Mallorys, she knew vaguely, had a yacht. And the note added to the envelope had been addressed to Tommy. It didn't take a genius to understand a possible connection between a yacht and $100,000 and a pinpoint on the coast just north of Veracruz.

If she were wise, she would try to reach the Consulate

in Guadalajara, but wisdom had never been her long suit. Why not get close to the action? She could take the note and the money to her cousin in Veracruz and let him alert the Mexican authorities there. And she would be in on the excitement.

"What the heck, Jack, you just live once," she said aloud and then, as the words seemed to linger in the little room, she shrugged a little. Perhaps that hadn't been the best phrase, but she didn't really care. She was Maura Kelly and she had always been game. She absolutely wouldn't scuttle to safety in Guadalajara. Somehow or other, she would make it to Veracruz and oh, would the trouble begin for Luis and Company!

She glanced again at the note. October 25. That would be Friday. This was Tuesday evening. She would go to Veracruz tomorrow and there would be plenty of time to arrange for interested spectators to gather at 20° 42' N, 96° 15' W.

Now, all she had to do was get to Veracruz with her exhibits, the message, that odd scrawled map added by Luis, and the money. And she wasn't going to carry them blithely along in her basket.

She pulled reflectively at her lip. She felt it necessary to conceal the money and the notes, and there was no point in kidding herself as to why. There was the chance she might be caught, either here in the District or in Veracruz. And, face it, if Luis got her, she could disappear without a trace because no one knew where she was or where she was going. Lin knew that she was in trouble, but she couldn't have any inkling what Maura intended to do.

For the first time, it occurred to Maura to wonder what Lin had told the *señora* and where everybody thought she was. Did she dare call? Well, what could it hurt? No one could find her over the telephone and she might get some hint from Lin as to what Luis and the Mallorys were up to. At the same time, she could tell Lin where she was going and, if Lin didn't hear from her by Thursday, ask her to notify the Embassy.

Swiftly, she dialed the house. Della answered.

"Hi, Della, this is Maura. May I speak to Lin, please?"

"Good heavens, Maura, are you calling all the way from Acapulco?"

Maura hesitated for only an instant. "Yes, and the water's fine. Is my roommate handy?"

"Nope, your very own glamor boy called up in a lather after dinner. Seemed he wanted your Acapulco address, at least that's what Lin said when she left."

Maura glanced at the clock on the desk. It was ten-thirty. She frowned. "How long has she been gone?"

"Oh, I guess she went out about eight. Do you want her to call you?"

"No, no. It's nothing too important." She thought quickly. "You see. I promised to find a quotation for her and I forgot to leave it at the house."

Della laughed. "You're a nut to spend money on a long distance call to talk about a quotation."

"I plead guilty, but do promise to tell her. It's for a class tomorrow."

"Sure thing. Fire away the deathless prose."

Maura hesitated, then, thinking as swifly as she could, she framed a quotation that would give Lin a hint as to her destination, but wouldn't sound too peculiar.

Della read the message back, then said, "Have a ball. See you this weekend."

Maura's smile slipped away as she put down the receiver. Why on earth had Lin gone out with Luis? But surely no harm would come to her. She didn't know enough to be in danger.

Maura picked up the note of instructions, the sketched

map and the stack of bills and carried them to the wicker divan. Just a little more to do and she could call it a night.

She retrieved her basket from the desk, put it on the floor by the divan and pulled out some of the purchases she had made that afternoon, the packet of needles, a small pair of scissors, a spool of strong black thread and the two *rebozos*.

She set to work, muttering occasionally as the threaded end of the needle pricked painfully against her unprotected third finger. She could almost hear her elegant grandmother pointing out that even the most inept of needlewomen did recognize the need for a thimble.

Once she put her sewing down in disgust and reheated the remaining coffee, but, when the cup was finished, she grimly set to work again. It was almost eleven when she finished. She stood and stretched, then walked to the desk. Her hand rested lightly on the telephone. Did she dare try to call Lin again? She picked up the receiver then slowly put it down again. She had left the message and, if she called again, someone might begin to wonder if she really was in Acapulco. She'd better leave well enough alone. And Lin must be all right. Luis would have no reason to harm her.

10
TRUST A NORTE

Lin sat in the noisy dance hall and watched as if mesmerized as the young Mexican came closer and closer. He moved unsteadily, stopping once to clutch the back of a chair for support. His friends at the bar hooted and he lowered his head and plunged forward again.

The girl gripped the edge of the table and then, panic tightening her throat, grabbed her purse and began to slide backwards along the bench.

Suddenly an arm dropped around her shoulders and a voice boomed, "Rosalia *mia,* I am so sorry I am late. My apologies could not be more abased."

As the flowing apology continued in loud Spanish, the drunken young man hesitated, then scowled and swung heavily around to walk back toward the bar.

"No luck tonight, Roberto," one of his friends cried. "Have another drink."

The young man shrugged, his good humor restored, and, sliding onto his seat at the bar, began to boast about other nights when his luck hadn't been so bad.

Lin's hand shook as she clutched Juan's arm. "Oh Juan, I was so afraid. How did you ever find me? Oh good grief, if you hadn't come . . . ." Her eyes darkened.

He leaned close and urged, "Smile, Lin, you must. Don't look frightened or worried. Act as if I am an old

Trust a Norte

friend. Come, play the part," and he threw back his head and laughed loudly.

She picked up her cue and laughed, too. Juan ordered for them again as if they had all the night and two men had not followed a terrified Luis from the room.

Under cover of a warm smile, she whispered, "Juan, can't we leave here?"

"In a moment. Let's dance once and then we'll go."

They danced cheek to cheek as did the others on the close-packed floor. Indeed, there wasn't room enough to dance any other way.

Juan whispered softly, "Keep on smiling. Don't look around. One of the men who came after Luis is standing at the bar. He's looking over the crowd. He sees us."

Lin stiffened in his arms.

"No," he cautioned. "Relax. Laugh."

She laughed and looked up into his face as if he had said something very clever, but her eyes were frightened and her smile strained.

He pulled her closer, kissed her on the cheek, and whispered. "It's all right. He's decided you were just a casual date of Luis'. He's going now. In a few minutes we'll leave."

Once outside, she took a deep breath and savored the wild crisp freshness of the air, but she didn't feel safe until they were in Juan's car and back on *Reforma,* far from that scruffy plaza and its dingy nightclubs.

"What about Luis?" she asked finally. "We can't just drive away."

Juan glanced swiftly at her. "Do not worry about him. I think he probably runs well enough."

Lin gave it up then. It was quite clear that Juan intended to do nothing about Luis and the tough looking men who had followed him.

She studied his profile as the car swept on out *Reforma,* past the Embassy and the Angel and the Diana and into *Chapultepec* Park. He looked so different from the goodnatured smiling boy she had enjoyed so much. His strong face was heavy in repose, almost stern.

And then she stiffened and sat up very straight. "Juan, I'm so grateful that you rescued me tonight, but how did you ever happen to be there?"

He was drawing a cigar from his coat pocket. His hand hesitated for a moment, then he clenched the cigar in his teeth. In a moment, when it was lit and drawing easily, he turned his head and smiled at her.

"I think your good angel guided me to the *Plaza Garibaldi* tonight. It isn't, I assure you, a customary hangout of mine, but some of the guys out at school asked me to take them around. I couldn't believe it when I looked up the square and saw you with Luis."

He glanced at her again, as if to gauge her reaction to his story.

"Perhaps I shouldn't have followed you," he said when she made no answer. "But I thought this was the fellow your roommate dated, the one who put the envelope beneath the clock at the *señora's*. I guessed you might be playing detective. I knew it wasn't any of my business, but that is a pretty rough area for nice girls so I decided it wouldn't hurt anything for me to keep an eye on you."

She shivered a little, partly from the chill night air, partly from the memory of that unsteady approach toward her table.

Juan reached across the seat to squeeze her hand, but it was a curiously perfunctory gesture. "I am glad now that I—how do you say it—followed my hunch."

"I'm glad, too," she said quietly, but her voice was drained and tired and it was an effort to press his hand in return. She wasn't quite as naive as Juan must think. She hadn't believed in good angels or fantastic coincidences in a long, long time.

She could almost hold in her hands the air of suspicion

in the small car, Juan's suspicion of her and her suspicion of him. She tried to think swiftly. What should she say? Whose side was Juan on? She wondered bitterly how many sides there were to this strange affair. She was sure of only one thing—she was on Maura's side.

It was Juan who broke the lengthening silence.

"I was a little surprised to see you with Luis. You told me that Maura intended to solve the little mystery of the note beneath the clock. I thought she would probably do her own sleuthing."

The car eased to a stop in front of the *señora's* house, but Lin scarcely noticed that she had arrived home. She turned and stared at Juan's shadowed face and wished that she knew him better. Was this some sort of ploy or didn't he know that Maura had run away? If he didn't know, maybe he had been in the *Plaza Garibaldi* by chance.

"Maura did do her own sleuthing," Lin said tiredly, "but she must have discovered more than she bargained for."

"What do you mean?" the Mexican asked sharply.

Again Lin paused warily. His tone revealed more than he realized. He was deeply, intensely interested in Maura and the message beneath the clock. Lin hesitated, then said evasively, "I don't really know what's happened, Juan. I think Maura must have intercepted a message under the clock. Anyway, somehow she discovered something dangerous about Luis. She is hiding somewhere. Tonight, Luis wanted me to come out with him. He said he had a message for me to give to Maura, but he didn't really. He thought I'd know where she was and he almost went to pieces when I convinced him I didn't know. He kept saying Maura had taken the money and *El Jefe,* whoever he is, wouldn't believe that she had taken it. He would think Luis had. None of it made much sense, except Luis was terribly frightened."

"He said Maura had taken the money?" Juan demanded.

Lin drew away from him. "That's what he said," she admitted uncertainly.

"If he doesn't find her then . . . ." He broke off sharply. "I think, Lin, you would be well advised not to play detective anymore." He paused, then spoke more gently, "I don't know what this is all about, but Luis must be involved in something dangerous."

"But what am I going to do?" she asked.

"Go in and go to bed." When she started to protest, he shook his head. "No, Lin, there isn't anything more you can do. Look, I'll check into this and see if I can find out something about this Luis . . . what's his last name?"

Lin looked at Juan expressionlessly. She felt sure that Juan was much more certain of Luis' last name than he was of her own. In a very dry voice she said, "Mendoza. Luis Mendoza."

"Yes, Luis Mendoza. Well, I'll see if I can find something out for you. Put it all from your mind."

"And Maura?" she asked. "Should I put Maura out of my mind, too?"

His face was unreadable. "I wouldn't worry too much about her. I think she must be very resourceful."

Lin was silent as they walked to the door. She liked Juan so much, but how could she trust him?

When they stood on the front steps, she almost told him all of it, about Maura's phone call and the sack and the Mallorys, but she didn't.

She held out her hand and said only, "Thank you, Juan, again, for coming to my rescue."

"I'm glad that I . . . happened to be there, Lin."

He said goodnight and turned away, then paused and faced her again. "Lin, please don't take any more chances. Don't try to find out any more."

In the dim light suffused through the windows of the common room, she half smiled. "I'll be careful, Juan. And thank you."

As the door closed behind her, Juan moved quickly down the steps. Once back in the car, he pulled a walkie-talkie case from beneath the seat, flicked it on and made his call. In soft Spanish he asked, "Where is Mendoza now?"

A voice replied gruffly, "We lost him. Him and his two pals."

Juan's shoulders slumped. *"Caramba,"* he swore bitterly. After a long moment, his face creased in concentration, he issued several sharp short orders, then turned off the walkie-talkie and returned it to its hiding place.

He drove off with a jerk, his thoughts black. One lousy American girl had loused it up, loused it all up, and to top it off, she was probably going to get killed in the process. Trust a *norte,* he thought, to louse everything up.

11
THE TRUE
CROSS

In the Alvarez house, Lin was climbing wearily up the stairs. Each step seemed too much to manage, but she finally reached the landing and walked slowly to her room. Pushing open the door she flicked up the light switch and stood there numbly. She wanted a bath. She wanted to wash away the lingering touch of that tawdry nightclub. And she wanted to wash away the film of fatigue that misted her thoughts. She must think tonight.

She felt completely confused. Luis and Juan and the Mallorys were somehow involved in whatever had driven Maura away. Somehow she must outwit them all, and find Maura. For a moment she wondered wildly how many people were involved in this dark secret. And she wondered what unlawful game they were playing. Was it dope running, jewel theft, kidnapping? Nothing seemed too melodramatic to consider after the day she had endured.

Still standing in the doorway, she looked dully around the room. It seemed alien tonight, without Maura.

Her gaze was caught by the white sheet of paper pinned to the pillow on her bed. It moved gently in the cool breeze from the still open casement window. In a flash, Lin was across the room. She pulled free the pin and spread the note open.

She read the message with puzzlement and dismay.

"Maura called from Acapulco, the dope. Said she promised to find a quotation for you. Here 'tis: 'The Irish seeks the true cross.' She said to tell you it's best read in Spanish. Isn't that just like the Red—off on a fling and she remembers to ring you about some dusty old quotation. Speaking of flings, where have you been tonight, lady?—Della."

Lin read it again and yet again but it made no better sense either time. How on earth could Maura have called from Acapulco? She had made that destination up out of nothing at the dinner table!

Lin sank down on her bed and wondered sickly if by some mischance she had hit upon Maura's true destination. She ran a hand through her thick tawny hair and then, slowly, her breath came easily again. Of course Maura hadn't gone to Acapulco or, if that was what she planned, she wouldn't stay there long. Maura hadn't disappeared so quickly and mysteriously to then announce to Della where she was.

She read the message again but the words seemed to waver before her eyes. And she must think! Dropping the note on the bed, she got up and hurried to the bath. After a quick shower, she did feel more alert. She pulled on her flannel nightgown and her soft fleece-lined slippers. Back in the room, she brewed a cup of instant coffee and sat down at the desk.

The Irish seeks the true cross. She printed the message on a sheet of paper and looked at it for a long time. Why would Maura say it was best read in Spanish? That didn't make any sense. It would, if translated properly, say the same thing in Spanish as in English. But Maura had specifically included that instruction.

Lin reached for her English-Spanish dictionary and quickly transcribed the message.

She studied the message both in Spanish and English.

The Irish could refer to either Maura or the Mallorys, but Lin decided it must mean Maura because the verb was "seeks" in the third person singular, not "seek." And the true cross. She began to say the words in Spanish and as they rolled off her tongue, she felt a flicker of hope. Vera cruz, Veracruz!

Maura must be going to Veracruz!

And then she sighed. Perhaps Maura was and perhaps she wasn't, but that was the best guess Lin could make.

She yawned then and put down her scratch pad. Tomorrow she would try to find out more, if she could. The Mallorys were her best bet. Somehow she would find out how the Mallorys were involved.

She switched off the light, dropped her robe in a chair and climbed into bed. She slept fitfully, waking once with her heart pounding until the mists of sleep parted and she knew she was safe in her own room and not braced against a wall in a tawdry room with a dark figure advancing unsteadily toward her.

Her breathing finally became deep and even as the gray dawn fingered through the shutters and she slept, free for the moment from worry and fear.

While Lin was finally drifting into sleep, Maura lay quietly in her borrowed bed and watched as the dim light of early day brushed away the shadows in the Dickinsons' apartment.

She waited until the thin gray light spread through the room, refining the shadowy masses of black into the couch and the chairs and the desk, then she thrust back the covers and swung out of bed. Shivering in the cold morning air, she quickly dressed, and in only a few minutes again surveyed a stranger in the mirror, the dark hair tucked into a bun on the neck, the black dress hanging limp.

She brewed strong black coffee and enjoyed two sharp

hot cupfuls. It took only a moment then to whisk away all traces of her visit, the bed neatly made, the dishes in place, the *Goode's World Atlas* back in the bookshelf.

Gathering up her basket, she wound the black *rebozo* around her shoulders and left.

She walked unhurriedly up the side street to *Reforma* and a slight smile curved her lips. It was the same half-expectant, half-challenging smile she wore when diving into a nine-foot wave or jumping a horse over a rushing stream.

It was a beautiful day, a perfect day. The soft shine of the sunrise touched stuccoed walls with gold. The sky was clear, unsmudged by the so often present smog, and as softly blue as a robin's egg.

She squeezed onto a second class bus, dropped 30 *centavos* in the coin box, and struggled toward the back. The bus rode heavily up the beautiful boulevard, passing the Angel and the Embassy and turned north on *Insurgentes,* swinging around the famous statute of *Cuauhtémoc,* the last of the Aztec kings who was taken prisoner and later killed by the Spaniards.

She moved closer to the rear door and a few blocks later got off the bus. The huge modern railroad station loomed up ahead, an imposing expanse of plate glass and shining gray marble.

Once within the great building, she crossed the wide expanse of smooth marble flooring to the ticket booths and bought her ticket for Train 52, the day train to Veracruz via Puebla, leaving at 9:05 a.m., arriving at 8:50 p.m. She glanced up at the wall clock. Half an hour to go.

As the train began to rumble free of the station, Maura took a deep breath, then regretted it a little as she inhaled a strong mixture of sweat, chicken (cackling in a box behind her), and mescal, held firmly in hand by a bearded man in blue denims. But she didn't really mind. It was a beautiful day, she had so far outwitted the opposition, and she was aboard a train. And she intended to enjoy every rumbling, wheel-clacking minute of it.

12
IN THE MALLORYS' APARTMENT

Lin waited in the musty darkness of the Alvarez garage, beneath the small apartment of the Mallorys, and felt three-fourths a fool. She looked down at her watch. Nine-thirty, and the Mallorys' VW still sat on the far side of the garage. Lin had slipped into the garage at a quarter 'til eight, planning to wait there until the Mallorys left, and then try to get into their apartment. But maybe they weren't going out to school all day. Maybe she would just moulder in this dingy converted stable with its pungent smell of gasoline and tires and rotting wood while the Mallorys gaily did crossword puzzles above.

And then she dropped into a crouch between the old Dodge sedan of *Señora* Alvarez and the rough wall of the garage. The Mallorys were clattering down the steps from the apartment above the garage.

The door squeaked on its sagging hinges as Tommy pulled it open. The bright widening shaft of sunlight spilled into the room, but it only deepened the darkness where Lin stood. She wondered just what she would say if either of them chose to come to this side of the garage. But she needn't have worried. The Mallorys were oblivious to everything but their soft-voiced yet violent quarrel.

RENDEZVOUS IN VERACRUZ

". . . absolutely crazy! We ought to take the first plane home!"

"Nothing doing," Tommy responded angrily. "Leave the boat and run home to Mother and Daddy, is that what you want to do?"

"Listen to me, Tommy," Natalie pled. "Please listen to me."

Lin carefully peeked up over the edge of the Dodge's fender.

Across the garage Tommy and Natalie looked at each other over the small humped top of the VW. Tommy's face was flushed and sullen, Natalie's pale and sad.

"Well, I just don't understand why you're so upset," he said defensively.

"Upset! What do you expect me to be? The phone rings and it's not Luis, it's somebody named Jaime who is calling for Luis, and this Jaime orders us, he doesn't ask, he orders us to meet him at the National Museum of Anthropology! Where's Luis, I'd like to know. It's his fault if the money didn't reach us, not ours."

Tommy slid his hand through his ruffled blond hair. "It doesn't make any difference who calls us," he said gruffly. "We have to go. We have to get that money. If we meet the freighter and we don't have the money . . ." His voice trailed off.

"Look," she said reasonably, "if we meet Mr. Stefanakos and we don't have the money for the shipment, it won't be our fault." She paused, then said in a rush, "Oh Tommy, let's sell our boat and then we can send the money to Mr. Stefanakos and we won't owe him a thing."

Tommy's shoulders sagged and he looked away from his wife.

"That's all we owe him, isn't it?" she asked again, but her voice was uncertain now.

Tommy didn't answer.

Natalie gripped the edge of the VW's roof, but when

In the Mallorys' Apartment

she spoke, her tone was gentle. "What is it, Tommy? What is it that you haven't told me?"

He looked at her, then quickly away. "He gave me a couple of thousand before we sailed." He paused, then added in a voice so low that Lin almost couldn't hear, "And he said if we double-crossed him, we wouldn't live to enjoy a penny of it."

Natalie stood there wordlessly for a long moment, then she opened the car door and slid in. Tommy swung into the driver's seat and, without another word spoken, he started up the little car and backed it roughly out of the garage.

Lin waited until the garage door swung shut and she heard the car move off down the driveway, then she straightened up from her hiding place. The cast was expanding, she thought soberly. Luis and Jaime and the Mallorys and now a Mr. Stefanakos. And it was all tangled up with a good deal of money, that Maura had somehow managed to intercept, and the Mallorys' boat.

Lin moved slowly away from the old car. Now, while the Mallorys were gone, it was time for her to find out more, if she could. But her legs seemed curiously unwilling to move. The aura of danger and fear that had surrounded the Mallorys sounded a very clear warning.

She walked reluctantly to the garage door and pushed it open. Stepping out onto the gravel, she turned and looked up at the stone staircase leading to the Mallorys' apartment.

This was the turning point, she knew. She could walk on past, go back to her room and get her books and hurry out to school.

She could do that.

The girl stood in the clear bright sunlight and thought of Luis' angry face the night before and of the Mallorys as they silently drove away—and of Maura, who was lighthearted and gay and very kind. And who was, Lin thought, decidedly outnumbered in this dangerous game.

Her legs trembled a little but she ignored them as she hurried to the steep stone steps and began to climb. At the top, she glanced around, but the driveway lay clear and empty. Turning, she twisted the doorknob. It was locked. She fished her house key out of her purse. It twisted in the lock.

Once inside, Lin shut the door firmly. As she waited for her quickened breathing to slow, she surveyed the small apartment. There wasn't much to see—a desk, a table, some chairs. A tiny kitchen and a bath opened across the room. Her gaze swung back and fastened onto a pinewood desk.

She crossed quickly to the desk and pulled open the shallow front drawer then looked in dismay at the welter of papers. Checkbook stubs mingled with a pile of maps. Two passports sat carelessly on top of a heap of bills. A dark blue book on navigation, a packet of sewing needles, a University bulletin, all this and more, much more.

She lifted and looked among the papers, trying all the while to replace everything as she had found it. Toward the back of the drawer, she found a small leather-covered book with Diary tooled in gilt on its cover.

Picking it up, she flicked through the pages, realizing quickly that it had been written by Natalie. She felt a quick distaste at reading someone else's private thoughts, but she continued grimly on, scanning each page. And then she stopped short and began to read in earnest.

June 8—Bought a converted caïque today. Tommy says it will be a ball to sail it back to Mexico, but I wonder how old the engine is!

This, Lin realized, must be the boat they had spoken of in the garage.

She turned each page carefully now, and followed the *Miranda's* voyage through the Mediterranean with stops

In the Mallorys' Apartment

at Bengasi and Tripoli and Tunis, then on through the Straits of Gibraltar and down the North African Coast, Rabat and Casablanca, Marrakesh and Agadir . . . .

Lin had been skimming the entries, the *Miranda's* difficulties with her diesel engine, the rotted sheeting of the mainsail that shredded into pieces in the near gale force winds that struck just past the Straits. And then the broken crankshaft and the arrival under makeshift sail at Agadir.

But she read carefully the entry for June 17: I wonder if we should accept any money from Mr. Stefanakos. He offered to help us last night and this morning Tommy has gone back to discuss the 'technicalities' of ordering a crankshaft.

The entry of June 18: Tommy says everything's all set. I asked him why Mr. Stefanakos would do this for strangers and Tommy said we might be able to help him out in a business way in Mexico. It's all very vague.

June 24: The crankshaft arrived yesterday and the engine is fixed. We should cast off in an hour. I'll be glad. I don't really like Mr. Stefanakos even though he certainly has been nice to us.

After that the entries were of days at sea and occasional stops in port. Lin began to skim again and almost missed the entry for July 29, but her eyes caught Mr. Stefanakos' name.

July 29: I finally had it out with Tommy and he admitted Mr. Stefanakos expects some return on the money he advanced us for the crankshaft. Tommy has promised to bring the *Miranda* out in October to meet a tramp freighter and bring some crates ashore. Tommy said it's some Roman art work from some excavations in North Africa and he's just helping Mr. Stefanakos avoid some red tape about the shipment of antiquities. I told Tommy that smuggling was smuggling no matter . . . .

The quick tiptap of high heels sounded on the stone

stairway outside. Lin shoved the dairy underneath some papers, slid the drawer shut and whirled to look desperately around the room.

The Mallorys were at the door now.

Lin half turned toward the kitchen. No, there was no cover there. An opened closet door showed it full to bursting.

She heard the click as Natalie unsnapped her purse.

Lin moved even as she looked over the room. Two straight chairs, a divan, a coffee table. It left no choices. She dropped to the floor and slid under the bed until she was hard against the wall.

The door swung open and Tommy and Natalie walked in.

Lin lay stiff and tense, and, for a moment, she couldn't really hear their voices over the thudding of her heart. She wondered that they didn't hear that frenzied thudding, but finally her pulse slowed and the words came clear.

". . . didn't do any good, did it, Tommy?"

"Sure it did," he replied irritably. "He understands that he won't get the shipment until we have the money in hand. And he's made it pretty clear they'll have the money by Friday."

A whoosh of running water sounded for a moment and then the acrid smell of a burnt match drifted out of the kitchen. Her voice a little muffled, Natalie inquired sarcastically, "And just how is dear old Jaime going to manage that? I suppose Maura is going to raise her hand and say 'Here I am' when he whistles for her."

"That's his problem," Tommy said.

"Is it, Tommy? What do you suppose Mr. Stefanakos will say Friday night when we rendezvous with him—and we don't have a dime in our jeans."

Tommy sat down heavily on the overstuffed divan. "It won't be our fault," he replied defensively.

In the Mallorys' Apartment

Natalie said no more, but the bangs and clatters from the kitchen testified to her temper. In a moment, she came out of the kitchen and thumped down a tray on the table.

"Let's eat," she said shortly. "I've fixed an avocado salad. Do you want your coffee now?"

"Doesn't matter," he said.

Chairs scraped and they sat down at the table. They ate in silence until, finally, Natalie put down her water glass with a sharp crack and said, "Oh Tommy, I can't stand this. Don't let's quarrel. We must talk this out."

He sighed. "Okay, Nat, but what good's talking going to do us?"

"I don't know, but we can't just blunder on. To begin with, what's in this shipment we are supposed to pick up?"

"Mr. Stefanakos explained all that," he began slowly. "It's a load of antiquities for a rich Mexican collector."

"Oh Tommy, you don't really believe that, do you?"

He pushed back his chair then. "Look, Natalie, it doesn't matter what I believe or even what's in the crates. In fact, we're better off the less we know. Let's just pick up those boxes, take 'em where we said we would and be like the three little monkeys. All right?"

"If you can promise me one thing," she said quietly.

"What?"

"Promise me it isn't dope. I won't do it, I won't touch it for all the money in the world if it's dope."

He laughed then, a shaky but relieved laugh. "I don't know what it is, baby, but it can't be snow because we could have brought that kind of stuff back this summer. No, this is something goodsized. We're supposed to bring on five crates and three smaller boxes."

Natalie let out a deep breath of air. "All right, Tommy. I guess if it isn't dope, it can't be anything too horrible." She paused and frowned, "But a hundred thousand dollars is an awful lot of money."

"Yeah, but these collecting nuts are willing to spend the earth to get something they want." He was suddenly gay. "Aw, come on, Nat, don't be a heavy. It's just a slick deal. I'll bet they find Maura and get the money back from her and everything will go like velvet."

"That's the other thing that worries me," his wife said soberly. "What will they do to Maura if they find her?"

He shrugged. "I don't know, but if she's going to go around lifting other people's money, she's going to have to expect trouble. Anyway, it's no skin off our nose. I'll tell you what, Nat, let's stop worrying about all of it. Let's go down to Veracruz right now. We need to get some work done on the *Miranda* if we're going out Friday night. And it'll be fun. How about it?"

Lin, absorbed, had crawled near the edge of the bed. Carefully, she peeked up from beneath the edge of the blanket.

Natalie was looking at her husband and her face was a Raggedy Ann mixture of sadness and affection. She smiled finally, but her eyes were misted. "All right, Tommy. We'll go to Veracruz."

Tommy pulled out a patched and faded cloth suitcase from the shelf in the closet and ebulliently began to pack. He swore goodnaturedly when he couldn't find his skin diving goggles. Natalie silently folded a few clothes into the case.

It took only a few minutes and then they were gone.

Lin waited until she heard the rumble of the VW starting up, then she inched out from beneath the bed. In only a moment more, she pulled shut the Mallorys' door behind her and started down the stone steps, a plan rapidly taking shape in her mind.

In the Mallorys' Apartment   117

13
ON TO
VERACRUZ

Lin packed swiftly and efficiently, a skirt and sweater, two blouses, a nightgown, socks, lingerie, sneakers, slacks and, after a moment's thought, her swim suit and cap. After all, she was scarcely off on a seashore holiday, but then she shrugged and let them be.

As she snapped shut her suitcase, she wished she could snap her thoughts into line as easily. But it is hard to be rock calm when you are just about to blow up your bridge behind you. And, if she carried out her plan, that would be precisely the effect. Unlike Maura, she couldn't whip off like a will-o'-the-wisp anytime she felt like wandering. The University rules were stringent. It took a letter of permission to leave town. Maura had one. She didn't. It was that simple.

So, if she went, she would probably end up expelled from the University. But, if she didn't go, Maura would be alone in trying to stop the Mallorys and Luis.

Maura's cryptic message ran through her mind: The Irish seeks the true cross. But not only Maura, Lin thought. All the Irish were seeking the true cross. The Mallorys were en route to Veracruz this minute.

Lin pulled her raincoat out of the closet and picked up her bag, then paused and laid them both on her bed.

RENDEZVOUS IN VERACRUZ

Her mind was made up. She was going to follow the Mallorys and try to find out what was going to happen aboard the *Miranda*. But there was no question in her mind that the venture lacked a little in safety.

Crossing to her desk, she pulled out two sheets of notepaper and, quickly, concisely, put down everything that had happened. When she finished, she sealed the sheets inside an envelope. Across it she scrawled: Della, open this if I don't call you on Sunday. Lin.

Downstairs she gave the note to Tina with instructions for her to give it to Della on Sunday and she pressed a ten-*peso* bill in the maid's hand.

Tina smiled and said, *"Si señorita,* I won't forget. The note to *Señorita* Della on Sunday."

"Oh, and Tina, do me a favor and tell the *señora* that I have been invited to accompany a group from the University to an archeological dig at Oaxaca and we won't be back until next week."

It was just possible, Lin hoped as she hurried down the walk, that her subterfuge might work. The *señora* might not check with the University because, after all, a school-sponsored field trip didn't require a letter of permission. And, if the *señora* didn't check with the school, then Lin might be able to make her unauthorized jaunt and get away with it.

She turned up *Prado Norte* toward *Reforma* and walked quickly, notwithstanding the suitcase. Head down, absorbed in her own thoughts, she paid no attention to the occasional traffic on the street. She knew she wouldn't find a cab until she reached *Reforma*.

The red VW squealed off *Reforma* onto *Prado Norte* and the whine of the wheels reflected the driver's irritation. "For Pete's sake, Nat, I *asked* you if you'd gotten the travelers' checks!"

"Well, I didn't hear you, Tommy. Anyway, it's not a major crime. We hadn't gone far." Her voice was quiet and tired.

Suddenly repentant, he said quickly, "I'm sorry, Nat, I didn't mean to gripe. I was just so glad to be getting . . . ."

He broke off suddenly and the pace of the car abruptly slackened.

"Well, well," he said softly. "Look across the street, Nat. Maura's little buddy is hiking along, suitcase in hand." His voice hardened, "And just what are the odds she's off to join her light-fingered friend."

Tommy pulled the car up to the curb and twisted to watch Lin walking up the street.

"What are we going to do, Tommy?" his wife asked unhappily.

"Follow her."

And it wasn't hard to do. The red VW tagged along after Lin's cab up *Reforma* then swung north on *Insurgentes* around the statue of *Cuauhtémoc*. Five blocks up *Insurgentes,* the cab turned right on *Buenavista.*

"So that's where she's going," Tommy said. "The ADO station."

Lin's cab pulled into the curb and a porter hurried up, hoping to carry her luggage.

The VW slid past and stopped at the corner. Tommy got out and Natalie moved over to the driver's seat. "Go around the block," Tommy directed. "I'll find out where she's going."

He waited until Lin disappeared inside the door to the bus station before he walked up. He looked through the plate glass windows and saw her in line before one of the ticket windows. The station was crowded but small. She would see him if he went inside. He hesitated, then beckoned to a porter and in his quick Spanish said engagingly, *"Señor,* I would like for you to get some information for me." He drew out his billfold and pulled free a 50-*peso* note. The porter's eyes fastened on it.

"I will be glad to help you, *señor*."

"Fine. Do you see the American girl in line for a ticket? There." Tommy pointed with the 50-*peso* note.

"Yes."

"Find out for me which bus she takes."

Tommy waited, leaning negligently against the rough stuccoed walls beyond the windows. The porter returned in only a moment.

"She takes the express bus to Veracruz, *señor*. It leaves at twelve o'clock and arrives in Veracruz at seven this evening."

Tommy handed him the money. "Thank you," he said. Turning, he hurried to the corner where the VW waited. As he got into the car, he said, "It gets interesting. Lin is going to Veracruz."

"To Veracruz!" Natalie exclaimed.

"Yeah and I'll bet that's where Maura is. Why else would Lin go down there? Come on, let's run back to the house. I can call Jaime and we can pick up the travelers' checks."

Natalie was quiet all the way back out *Reforma*.

She spoke once, quietly, "I wish you wouldn't call him."

Tommy shot an angry glance at her. "For Pete's sake, why not?"

"Because they'll catch Maura."

"Well, that's what we want them to do!"

"What do you suppose will happen when they catch her?" Natalie asked.

He shrugged. "So who cares? She should have thought twice before picking up a hundred grand that didn't belong to her."

"Oh Tommy, please don't call Jaime!"

On to Veracruz   121

He drove faster. "You should worry a little more about us and a little less about that redhead. Have you thought about what may happen if we make that rendezvous and we don't have the money with us?"

She looked out the window and didn't answer. When the VW careened into the Alvarez driveway and slewed to a stop by the garage, she waited quietly in the car. In only a few minutes, Tommy hurried down the stone steps and slammed into the car. He tossed the travelers' checks to Natalie and she dropped them into her purse without a word.

They were speeding along *Insurgentes* before she finally asked, "What did Jaime say?"

Tommy started grimly down the road. "He said he'd put out an alert for Maura. He said they'd catch her, all right."

They were on the outskirts of town when Natalie turned to him and clutched his arm and softly pled, "Tommy, let's chuck the whole thing. When we get to Veracruz let's provision the *Miranda* and sail to New Orleans. Please, Tommy."

He drove on and the sandy dry land of the valley of Mexico flashed past. He pulled out to pass a diesel truck on the upgrade of a hill then jammed his brakes and swung back into his lane just in time as a car came over the rise.

The miles clicked away and still he made no answer. "Tommy, we could do it. We could."

He looked at her briefly, despair in his face, then once again fastened his gaze on the highway. "No, Nat. We don't dare. I took that money from Mr. Stefanakos and he would find us. I don't care how far we ran or how fast. He would find us. And there's Luis and Jaime and somebody called *El Jefe*. Jaime made it pretty clear what *El Jefe* will do if we don't play ball."

The girl looked at him sombrely. "Luis and Jaime and

El Jefe," she repeated slowly. "Who are they? Can you tell me again and believe it that we're only smuggling in antiquities to avoid red tape? Antique collectors don't play that rough, Tommy."

He hunched his shoulders and stared grimly ahead. "I don't know what we are going to bring in, Nat. And I don't want to know."

Lin checked her suitcase then sat on a hard brown bench and waited for her bus to be called. It was warm in the small station, warm with people and with movement. She looked around the crowded room and saw so much of Mexico. A barefoot Indian in a worn but brilliantly patterned *serape* moved about with a fistful of lottery tickets, chanting his spiel. An old woman from the country with all her life collected in a bundle of newspaper and strapped cardboard boxes lay asleep on the floor, her careworn hands turned palms up. Two nicely dressed Mexican women chatted softly. A girl younger than Lin soothed a crying baby. And everywhere, people moved back and forth, standing in line for tickets, carrying boxes and baskets or smoothly expensive suitcases. And above the soft mumble of voices the tinny address system sounded out the imminent departure of buses. Buses for Pachuca, for Orizaba, for Oaxaca and then, for Veracruz.

Lin filed through the door to the bus. She glanced down at her ticket. Seat No. 10. She smiled to find it beside the window.

The bus trundled heavily out *Insurgentes* but began to pick up speed as the city dwindled. Lin looked back as they neared the hills which rimmed the city and saw, spreading away in the distance, the Valley of Mexico, where the gleaming city of the Aztecs had beckoned to the invading Spaniards.

The bus plunged along the asphalt road past squat-roofed settlements. An occasional church dome, its paint faded and peeling, thrust above the wide flat countryside. Horse-drawn plows furrowed through pebblestrewn arid soil.

The mountains surrounding the central plateau hulked against the horizon, huge mounds of rugged upthrust earth. And then the bus was upon the range and the road edged rocky gorges. *Saguaro* and prickly pear cactus clung tenaciously to the hillsides.

Every so often, the bus would rumble, its speed undiminished, by a cluster of houses. One-room adobe huts with old pieces of tin for roofs contrasted with the occasional *hacienda,* set far back from the road, whitewashed walls gleaming bright in the sunlight.

Lin watched through the window, entranced as the miles rolled past. The road began to climb again, up and around pine blanketed hills. Cultivated valleys slanted between the hills, every usable foot terraced for planting corn.

The pines grew taller and thicker and the air cold. As the bus rumbled over a bridge women below looked up from their wash then bent again to the age-old task of cleansing clothes in icy rushing water. Other clothes, clean now, lay spread atop thick prickly bushes to dry.

The road curved by tiny settlements and larger villages, past thatched peaked roof huts and one-room adobe homes with slits for windows, through a lovely small town with a bright central square.

The mountains gave way to cactus-studded desert with the humps of more mountains bone gray in the distance. Lin watched through half closed eyes, soothed by the silence and the steady pace. The landscape finally blurred before her eyes, a sepia canvas blotched irregularly with rows of green maguey.

She woke when the bus lurched to a halt in the town of Alchichica and she knew they were well past the desert.

RENDEZVOUS IN VERACRUZ

Adobe buildings slanted on a hillside and the air bit sharp and cold when the travelers straggled out of the bus into a modest roadside restaurant.

Lin enjoyed a bowl of chicken soup and a bottle of purified water. She realized that she had been hungry, but when she glanced at her watch, she was startled to find it was already four o'clock. And the bus would reach Veracruz at seven.

Once underway again, she relished anew the wonderful variety of Mexico. The land was now all hills, rich and cultivated. Clouds drooped close to the earth and the occasional wreath of wood smoke spoke of warmth and homes. The hills rose to mountains and the great fir trees loomed majestically above the roadway. Rich black dirt hosted cornfields. And once, close by the road, a cemetery flashed by, the stones gleaming white or pastel blue or rich rose.

As the late afternoon sun flooded the countryside, she continued to watch the changing world outside her window, tobacco leaves drying in racks along a field's edge, sugar cane swaying in the light breeze and everywhere wild flowers and vines, flowers the color of gold and ruby, vines thick enough to match a man's arm.

And finally, not bothering to look at her watch or the sun low in the west, she knew Veracruz was near. The wealth of the tropics spread across the land, orange and lemon groves, avocado trees and coconut palms.

The day had rushed past, a kaleidescope of color and beauty and contrast, and she hadn't thought at all about the journey's end. But now, think she must.

14
A HUT IN THE JUNGLE

Maura peered out into the darkness, watching as the haze of light far ahead began to separate into clusters of brightness—Veracruz at last. The last few miles the rhythm of the wheels seemed to echo the name, Veracruz, Veracruz, Veracruz.

As the train rumbled slowly into the station, she picked up her basket and moved down the aisle, eager to be off, impatient to reach the Consulate and be done with this odd interlude, this strange excursion into danger.

Danger seemed very distant when she stepped down from the vestibule. A vendor of hot shrimp made his way through the debarking passengers and Maura almost waved him down, then smiled and walked quickly on. She would have plenty of time for the minutes-fresh succulent shrimp of Veracruz, but first she must finish her adventure.

She hurried through the big old station with its dark wooden benches and general air of gloom, so different from the bright and shiningly modern station in the District.

Once outside she paused long enough to breathe deeply of the soft sea air, then she struck off down the street, softly lighted by street lamps. On her right rose the monument to Don Benito Juárez, the great Mexican leader who fought against foreign domination. She passed the Post and Telegraph Office and the Maritime Building.

And with each step, her spirits lightened. She felt no press of time, no fear. She was on her way. And, as she neared the *Malecón de Paseo*, it was all so familiar, so reassuring. Street lamps illuminated the fronts of the little shops along *Landera y Coss*. Straw purses, polished shells, woven baskets, leather belts, silver trinkets, all these glittered in the windows or spread out onto the sidewalk to entice the holidayers down early for a weekend by the sea.

She turned left on the *Malecón*, the boardwalk leading to the boulevard, *Avila Camacho*, that skirts the sea for miles along the bay. And as she turned she could see the bay, darker even than the night.

Her pace increased. Almost there. Almost there. Her footsteps seemed to sound the phrase. Without realizing it, she stood straighter, walked freer, her arms swinging in rhythm with her quickened pace.

She turned right, passing by the modern Bank of Mexico, all glass and concrete. And then, a block away, she could see her goal, a modest white stuccoed building. The flag was down, of course, but she knew the Consul lived with his family in the quarters behind the offices.

In only a moment, she would be inside and the Consul would call Ben and everything would be all right. She surged ahead. She was cutting across the street, angling toward the stone steps leading up to the door, when the call came.

"Maura, hey Maura!"

She was Maura Kelly and she was almost at the Consulate. She half turned to her right, a smile on her face, and that was her mistake.

A man, half sitting, half lying against the tufted bark of a nearby palm tree, rolled to his feet with astonishing swiftness.

A Hut in the Jungle   127

As he moved, Maura lunged toward the Consulate but he was between her and the steps. Quickly she was enveloped in a *serape,* picked up and flung into the back seat of an old Ford that had begun to roll forward even as she responded to the call. The door slammed shut. The Ford careened around the corner. In a moment even the tail lights were lost in the distance.

A middle-aged American woman stared in puzzlement at the now empty sidewalk in front of the Consulate.

"Ralph, did you see that, Ralph?"

Ralph, who had been enjoying the passage of young and darkly lovely girls, harumphed, and said, "See what, Mabel?"

His wife frowned. "Oh, nothing, I guess," she said uncertainly. "I do hope that girl wasn't sick. They seemed to be carrying her."

The Sanchez family, hard at work in their improvised fruit stand on the boardwalk by the sea, didn't see it at all.

The Mexican businessman on a holiday with his family paused in midstride. He wondered who the women was, then shrugged and walked on. An affair of the heart, no doubt.

In the speeding Ford Maura struggled to free herself from the *serape,* which was scratchy, smelly and probably vermin infested. The woolen blanket was abruptly yanked free and, in the fleeting light from a street lamp, she looked into the cold black eyes of Luis, eyes in a face almost unrecognizable. She pulled back against the seat. She managed to sit tall and straight but a wave of sickness washed over her.

He held a Luger in his hand and the long barrel was even with her mouth. He slowly moved it forward until the steel pushed against her lips.

"Don't move. Don't scream. I would shoot you now if I didn't have orders to bring you to the chief."

Light swept again across his face and Maura winced.

His mouth twisted. He pushed the gun a little harder against her mouth until she could feel the pressure on her teeth.

"It bothers you some?" he asked softly. "My face? It should. They didn't believe me at first when I said I didn't take the money. The chief has a man, Francisco, who likes to persuade people to talk. It made him sad when the chief finally believed me. Maybe he will let Francisco ask you some questions."

She pulled her head back until the muscle in her neck ached, but still the gun pressed against her, harder and harder.

"Basta de tonterías, Luis."

The sharp rebuke from the driver evoked an angry mutter from Luis but, after a long moment, the pressure against her mouth eased and he slowly drew the gun away.

Maura quietly drew a deep breath and looked with gratitude at the back of the driver's head and then she swung into attack.

"It is all nonsense!" she said sharply. "I don't even know what you are talking about. I didn't take anybody's money!"

Luis' body tensed and as swiftly as the flick of a whip he slapped her.

Maura's head jolted back against the cushion, but through the shock of pain she heard the driver warn Luis to knock it off.

Maura sat up straight again and repeated huskily, "I don't know what you're talking about."

Luis made no answer but stared blankly ahead as the car's headlights swept up the coastal road, free now of Veracruz.

The girl pulled as far away from Luis as possible and looked at the driver. He had saved her from Luis' anger but only so she could be delivered in prime condition to the 'chief,' whoever he might be.

For a moment her shoulders slumped. She had no illusions about how long she could hold out if the chief and his Francisco decided to be persuasive. She couldn't outlast them, but perhaps she could outwit them.

"Who is the chief?" She asked the question at large.

Neither Luis nor the driver responded.

She waited a moment, then asked archly, "For heaven's sake, can't I even know who I'm going to talk to? The chief. Chief of what?"

Luis responded sulkily, "You might as well come off it, Maura. It's not going to do you any good. 'Chief of what,'" he mimicked. "I'll tell you what he's chief of. The toughest, most dangerous band of bandits in eastern Mexico."

"A bandit chief!" she repeated in disbelief. "Now you're putting me on, Luis."

"Oh no, I'm not," he said angrily. "Why he's . . . ."

"*Bastante,*" the driver said curtly and again Luis subsided.

Maura, too, was quiet. A bandit chief. That didn't make any sense at all. Obviously, she had intercepted instructions for the landing of some smuggled goods into Mexico. But bandits aren't smugglers. They rob. They kill if anyone is foolish enough to oppose them. But they don't smuggle. That was the province of slick city crooks and even slicker financiers who smuggle blacklisted materials from Western countries to behind the Iron Curtain.

Bandit chiefs don't smuggle.

Maura almost challenged Luis, then thought better of it. She looked out the window but the moonless night masked the way.

In a few minutes the car slowed. Maura stiffened to attention, but the car didn't stop. It turned right on a dusty narrow road. Thick tropical growth met above the road, hiding the brilliance of the stars and there was only the rutted country lane, illuminated by the headlights.

They drove in silence, on and on. The road curved and twined through the jungle growth. The old Ford bucketed along the pitted road until, suddenly, with no apparent change in the scenery, nothing to mark this stretch of road as different from any other, the car slowed and abruptly swung to the right onto what was little more than a faint track into the jungle.

The going was slow now. The roar of the motor seemed louder in the narrow tunnel beneath the thick leafed trees. And the car jounced to a stop in a clearing hardly large enough to qualify for the name. The driver turned off the motor and the lights and in the sudden dark and silence the sense of movement and sound of the living jungle pressed into the car, filling it with a soft and alien presence.

"End of the line," Luis said harshly. "Get out."

Maura didn't move.

"This is fantastic!" she said angrily. "Where on earth are we?"

"A long way from the American Consulate," Luis retorted and he prodded her with the Luger.

The driver got out. A huge flashlight in hand, he flicked it on, pinned Luis in its beam and said sharply in Spanish, "Put it up. Or does the little boy need his toy to feel so big?"

Luis' face flushed. The Luger wavered in his hand and then, sullenly, he shoved it in his belt.

Ignoring Luis, the driver looked at Maura. "Out, *señorita.*"

Maura slowly got out of the car.

The driver turned and walked rapidly away.

Now there, Maura thought as she trudged after him,

was a man who expected to be followed and was, therefore, followed. Should she live so long, she might profit
by his example.

The clearing ended abruptly but the man didn't hesitate. He led the way along a faint path. Vines hanging
from branches overhead flicked across them as they
walked. The air was warm and cloying, thick with the
sweet smell of rotting vegetation, grown up so quickly
in the rich moist soil but blocked from the sunlight by
trees and tall bushes.

They walked, the man easily and surely, Maura and
Luis clumsily, for a good fifteen minutes. And then
abruptly they stopped. The man flicked out the light and
whistled softly three times. Out of the darkness someone responded with an equally soft whistle, then called
in Spanish, "Jaime, come on ahead."

The light on once again, they walked down a slope,
the trees and bushes thinning and stopped by a thatched
hut near the edge of a slow moving rippling river.

The hut, built of bamboo with a palm leaf roof, was
only a few yards from the river and a narrow dock.

Jaime pushed open the plank door, which was makeshift but, Maura noted, very solid. He motioned her
within.

She stood in the threshold and in the light of the torch
saw that the hut was empty of all but the most meagre
possessions. A woven grass mat lay rolled up near a stone
hearth. A handleless basket filled with wooden chips and
dried grass sat near a *metate,* the traditional three-legged
stone mortar for the grinding of corn.

But the most cheerful sight in a noticeably grim
evening was the flicker of fire in the hearth and the small
pot suspended on sticks over the flame. Its contents
bubbled softly and smelled wonderful.

"You will stay here, *señorita.*"

"How long?"

"Until *El Jefe* can come."

"And when will that be? I'll be glad when I can prove this has all been a mistake."

Jaime shrugged. "I hope you can convince him so, *señorita*, but *El Jefe* is a very smart man."

"Will he come tonight?" she asked.

"No."

He turned to the man who had welcomed them to the hut and a rapid exchange in Spanish followed.

Maura held her face still and blank but she listened intently. The man, called Ramón by Jaime, said the chief had sent word that he would be waiting for Jaime the next afternoon by the abandoned Morelos *hacienda*.

Jaime looked at Maura. "You must be patient, *señorita*. I will return with *El Jefe* tomorrow night or by Friday at the latest."

"Thursday night or Friday!" she exclaimed. "But I am expected now, tonight, by my father's cousin who works in the Consulate in Veracruz."

If she expected mention of the Consulate to worry Jaime, she quickly realized it bothered him not at all.

"Then he must be disappointed, *señorita*," Jaime repied easily. "You will not be uncomfortable here. There is a fine *guisado*, a stew, cooking. You will find water in the jug. *Buenas noches, señorita*."

He turned to go, then swung around. "Oh, *señorita*, please do not try to leave the hut. Ramón will be on guard outside."

And he was gone. Luis with him, she supposed. The door was pushed shut and she heard the latch fall into place.

The light on the hearth flickered in the draft of air from the closing of the door. She knelt by the fire and added two more chips of wood. In the sharp spurt of firelight her face was somber and tired.

She picked up a wooden spoon resting on one of the

hearth stones and gently stirred the stew. It did smell marvelous. She dished some up in a pottery bowl and, as she waited for it to cool, she wondered what on earth she was going to do.

15
LIN FINDS THE MIRANDA

Lin sat at her ease in the sidewalk café and savored both her second cup of cappuccino, that wonderful mixture of coffee and milk and spices, and the tropical beauty and charm of Veracruz.

Brilliant sunlight poured over the *Plaza de Armas,* with its flowering shrubs and coconut palms and bright pink flowers. To her left the Municipal Palace glittered, a dazzling white. Across the *Plaza* she could see the cream-colored Parochial Church, old and stately and gently aged. To her right rose the dignified and old-fashioned *Diligencias* Hotel. It too had an arcaded sidewalk café.

Lin smiled. The balmy air, the brilliant colors, the indefinable aura of a seaside resort, all combined to create a sense of ease and sureness. The night before, when when she had arrived at her hotel after dark, tired and worried, she had eaten with little thought of enjoyment and retired to her room to pace back and forth, convinced that her trip was pointless, that she could do nothing to help Maura.

But now, at shortly after eight on Thursday morning, everything seemed different. She was rested. She had slept deeply and dreamlessly, perhaps in part because of the drop from 7,000 feet to sea level. She had breakfasted magnificently. And she was surrounded by beauty.

She knew she should get started but it was hard in the relaxed atmosphere to recapture the sense of urgency that had goaded her to Veracruz. She watched the people go past. The sidewalks were full, schoolgirls in their uniforms, businessmen with briefcases, holidayers in sports shirts, shoeshine boys and street vendors, but no one seemed harried or hurried.

Lin wished suddenly, sharply, that she had come to this old and lovely port city for fun alone, to listen to the cheerful vibrant tones of the marimbas, to swim in the soft warm water of the Gulf, to enjoy the famed *huachinango a la Veracruzana,* red snapper with onions, peppers, olives and capers.

But all things seemed possible this beautiful morning. She would find out what the Mallorys were going to do; then she would go to the police and let them handle it.

She frowned and tried not to think how much she liked the Mallorys. Pushing away her empty cup, she signaled the waiter. After paying the check, she turned to her left and walked briskly up the sidewalk, her goal the harbor. At *Coss* street, she turned right, passing little trinket and shell and basket shops, and she could see the broad *Malecón de Paseo* which leads to the harbor.

When she reached the *Malecón,* she could glimpse the sea and her pace quickened. At the end of the broad tiled walkway, she stopped and leaned against the stone parapet to look at the wide expanse of the bay. The Fortress of *San Juan de Ulúa* sat gray and forbidding on a spit of land to the left. Closer at hand sunlight sparkled on all kinds of ships, a rusted black oil tanker, a sleek Mexican Coast Guard vessel, even a gleaming white freighter flying the Hammer and Sickle. At a nearby slip, stevedores loaded massive cartons onto a Norwegian freighter while across the bay, berthed at a refinery, a creamy yellow British ship took on a load of oil.

She could have watched the shifting scene all day but finally, reluctantly, she turned onto the Boulevard *Avila Camacho,* which skirts the bay for miles. She passed the tall modern Bank of Mexico and at the next corner paused for a moment to look at the small white Consulate with Old Glory fluttering on the flagpole mounted above the front door.

She knew it wasn't far now to the Yacht Club. The desk clerk this morning had told Lin that the Yacht Club was the likeliest place for Americans to moor a boat.

As carefully as she counted the next few blocks, she almost passed the place right by without recognizing it. Somehow, the very words Yacht Club had conjured up an impressive picture and she found the Yacht Club to be a very modest place. The small modern structure, built out on piles over the water, looked deserted. And, instead of a flock of boats, Lin counted only nine craft anchored nearby. They ranged in size from a tiny one-man sailboat to a huge powercruiser.

Lin lurked behind a palm tree, ready to cut and run, but she saw no familiar faces. If Tommy and Natalie were aboard one of the boats, they must be below. So Lin relaxed a bit and drew closer to the parapet. She was studying the boats, wondering which might be the *Miranda,* when a small boy about twelve leaned against the parapet beside her. She looked down at him questioningly.

"Are you looking for friends, *señorita?* Can I be of service to you? My name is Miguel."

Lin smiled at him. "I'm not looking for anybody, Miguel, I'm just admiring the boats. But maybe I could hire you to be my guide for awhile."

"O.K., what do you want me to show you?"

"I'm interested in the boats," she explained. "Can you tell me what kinds they are and everything?"

"Sure I can," he said proudly. And tell her about the

boats, he did. All about the sleek white yacht that be-
longed to a Bolivian mine owner, the graceful British
yawl that had won every race she had run, and the what
seemed to Lin incredibly tiny one-man sailboat whose
owner was making a round the world voyage.

It took only a single question to find out which boat
was the *Miranda*.

"What kind of boat is that?" she asked, pointing to the
white wooden boat with a broad stern and uplifted prow.

"It is a Greek boat but it belongs to an American and
his wife. The *señor* said it is called a caïque. They are
sailed on the Mediterranean. This one has a single cyl-
inder diesel engine and can make seven to nine knots."

Lin tried to nod intelligently although she wouldn't
know a diesel if she fell over it.

"It looks awfully big for two people to sail," she said.

Miguel shrugged. "It is not so easy, the *señor* said, but
not so hard if you know how. He told me she is forty-five
feet long and weighs twenty tons. She once was used for
sponge fishing but someone brought her in Greece a long
time ago and made her into a—how do you say—a boat for
fun?"

"A pleasure boat," the girl responded.

"Yes, a pleasure boat. She has lots of room aboard.
Would you like to see her?"

"Oh no," she said hastily. "I wouldn't want to bother
the people who own it. I mean, they wouldn't want a
stranger coming on board."

"No sweat," he said, and she could see that he was
very proud of the phrase. "No sweat," he repeated.
"They've gone to market. I said I would go for them, but
the lady laughed and said they liked to go and would
spend the morning. So I can take you aboard."

Normally Lin wouldn't have considered going aboard
anyone's boat uninvited, but normally she wouldn't be

searching for a fugitive roommate or trying to trap two likeable smugglers.

She didn't hesitate at all. Or at least only long enough to ask, "Are you sure they'll be gone all morning? I shouldn't like to be caught aboard."

"We'll make it," Miguel said eagerly. "Come on, let's go."

He took her arm and led her toward the gate barring entrance to the boardwalk leading to the Yacht Club.

"How're we going to get on board?" she asked, holding back. "We can't go into the Yacht Club. Somebody will stop us."

"Nobody's there right now. Old Pedro, the caretaker, is across the way drinking coffee."

Lin followed him, looking nervously over her shoulder. Once through the dim quiet club and on the slender pier behind it, she breathed a little easier. However, it didn't bear thinking about should the Mallorys return before she and Miguel finished their illicit expedition. She would, she supposed, just slither quietly over the edge of the pier.

The *Miranda* was moored near the end of the pier. When she and the boy reached the gangplank, she did feel a moment's compunction, but only for a moment. The Mallorys were showing no compunction about violating the laws of the country which had made them welcome. Lin owed them no courtesy.

She and Miguel crossed the small gangplank and dropped to the deck. The deck has been freshly hosed that morning and the worn wood was clean and sparkling. She looked around the afterdeck and realized that a lot of love and care had been put into the boat. The cockpit housing and the small forward wheelhouse had been painted a light blue and this morning matched the glowing tropical sky.

Lin Finds the Miranda   139

Miguel showed her the length of the boat from the engine astern to the cockpit housing to the mast to the wheelhouse. They returned to the afterdeck and, with one more searching glance to shore, Lin followed Miguel through the open doors of the cockpit housing down below deck.

It was amazing to the girl how much room there was below, two cabins, a saloon with a small couch and two chairs, and, up forward, a galley with a dinette opposite. She explored the cabins and realized there was much more room than the Mallorys used. One of the cabins was obviously a catch-all storage space.

After a last quick look around the rest of the *Miranda,* she urged Miguel topside. Once through the Yacht Club and back on the sidewalk, she breathed a sign of relief, gave the boy ten *pesos* and thanked him for her tour.

As she turned to go, he called out, "You come back anytime, miss. I will take you around again for free."

"Thank you, Miguel." She started to retrace her steps of the morning, then stopped and swiftly turned in the opposite direction. The Mallorys were coming up the street!

Her heart didn't stop thudding until she was a good two blocks beyond the Yacht Club, even though she was sure they hadn't seen her. She hoped to heaven that Miguel would keep his mouth shut. Why hadn't she thought to warn him! And then she realized that he would be no more eager to have anyone know of their clandestine visit to the *Miranda* than she.

Somewhat reassured, she walked more slowly. She was nearing the beach area for swimming. She picked out a café at random, one built out on piers over the water. She sat at the very rear at a small table that overlooked the water and, as she waited for her fish soup and coffee, watched the changing hue of the water from the sandy gray shallows to the gleaming turquoise depths. The occasional waves were thin and low-crested, the ocean's surge tamed and weakened by the extensive breakwaters.

She was almost finished with her soup before she felt steady again. As she sipped her coffee, she stared out grimly over the water and wished that she had the sort of temperament that would think it a lark to board a boat uninvited and then almost stumble into the owners. Unfortunately, even thinking about her near miss with the Mallorys made her hands tremble. She clenched her coffee cup a little tighter. If she carried through with the scheme which had suggested itself to her on the boat, she would darn well have to develop some temperament.

She spent the afternoon shopping and it took quite a while to find everything she would need if she did attempt her scheme. Back in the hotel room, she spread her purchases out on the bed and checked over the motley collection—a black turtleneck sweater, black slacks, a waterproof flashlight, a compass with a fluorescent dial. She looked at the compass with no fondness. If it came to the point that she was dependent upon a compass to see her home, she probably wasn't coming home again.

Turning away, she crossed to the shutters, pulled them open and stepped out onto the narrow balcony. The lights were flickering on around the plaza and a gentle breeze rattled the palm fronds. The plaza was beginning to fill and she realized, looking toward the Municipal Palace, that a band was setting up on the wide balcony. There would be a concert soon. The girl smiled and leaned against the wooden balustrade. Families settled on the grass, young couples sat close together on the marble benches. An occasional sailor on shore leave, vendors with balloons and toy airplanes and fruits, relaxed Mexican tourists, they all milled about, ready to enjoy a balmy evening at a seaside resort.

She swung around into her room and grabbed her purse. Her plans were made, her purchases complete. There was nothing more to be done until tomorrow. Tonight, she would join the holidayers.

And she had a lively evening. After a marvelous lobster dinner and sweet chocolate for dessert, she joined the throng in the plaza and for an hour listened to the martial strains of the band. When the concert ended, she boarded an open air trolley and rode all the way out of town to a beach hotel and back again. And when she finally reached her room at a quarter 'til eleven, she was relaxed and buoyant and thoroughly happy.

Smiling to herself and humming a gay little tune, she slipped her key into the lock and swung open the door. Stepping inside, she pushed the door shut behind her.

As it clicked closed, she stopped in mid-stride and her heart began to thud, that old familiar pound of fear. Half turning, she opened her mouth to scream. A strong arm closed around her shoulders and a hand shut painfully hard over her mouth.

RENDEZVOUS IN VERACRUZ

16
"DON'T SCREAM!"

"Don't scream!" he whispered urgently. "For the love of heaven, don't scream!"

Her heart pounded and her lungs felt as if they would burst, but the low whisper reached her and slowly her taut muscles relaxed. The pressure against her mouth eased then fell away entirely.

She leaned limply back against him. It was a long moment before she felt strong enough to turn and say shakily, "Juan, didn't your mother ever tell you to knock on a lady's door?"

At his soft, quickly smothered laughter, she was completely reassured.

He grasped her hand. "I'm sorry, Lin, truly I am. I didn't mean to scare you. I had to grab you because I could tell you were going to scream before I'd have a chance to let you know it was me."

She turned on the light, then crossed to the wicker chair by the bed and dropped into it. Her legs still felt too unsteady to remain standing.

"Now that I know it's you, my friend, I'd be interested to know why," she said. "I think I can be safe in assuming that you aren't lurking in my room at this hour to play a friendly game of poker."

He replied equably, "No, I'm not. But I'm also equally sure that you aren't in Veracruz for the fine salt air."

They stared at each other warily.

It was Juan who broke the silence. "Turn off the light and come here," he said, crossing to the shuttered door to the balcony.

She hesitated, then obeyed. He opened the shutter just a little and pointed down toward the Plaza. "See those men?" he asked. "The young tough having a beer on the sidewalk by the *Diligencias*? And the older man with gray hair, sitting on that park bench?"

She looked down and saw them and her skin prickled. The boy and the man, their faces were familiar. The boy had eaten lunch at the same pier café. Once while shopping that afternoon, she had changed her course and turned abruptly back the way she had come and had startled the man behind her. The same man now sat at his ease on a plaza bench. And only a little while ago, she had half noticed the boy on the trolley.

Lin turned toward Juan and in the soft shaft of light through the partially opened shutter, her face was pale and set.

"Your watchers?" she asked coldly.

"No, not mine. My man's over there in the shadow of the Municipal Palace."

She was both angry and frightened now. She slammed the shutter closed, crossed to the light, and flicked it on. And then she turned to look across the room at Juan.

"You are having me watched and so is someone else!"

He smiled but no smile reached his eyes. Bright and unreadable, they watched her intently.

"Who are you?" she demanded abruptly.

"Juan Borja," he replied.

She looked at him, her eyes sad and questioning. "But you aren't what you seem to be," she said slowly. "You aren't just a Mexican at the University of the Americas to study English literature."

He stared back impassively at her.

"You were in Veracruz last month," she said emptily. "And a man tried to knife you."

"How did you? . . . Oh, George Hammond, he told you. Right?"

She shrugged. "He told Maura and she told me. Why were you here, Juan?"

"I was here on business. The same business that brings me to Veracruz tonight."

"And what is that? What is it that brings you after Luis and Maura and whoever else is involved?"

"Whoever else is involved," he repeated slowly. "That is the real question. You ask who I am but I cannot say until I am sure that you are indeed who you appear to be."

She frowned. "What do you mean? Of course I'm who I say I am."

"Just a student, then. A simple nice American girl. That is what you say. And that is what I believed. But yesterday you came to Veracruz. Why?"

"You don't think it's a coincidence?" she asked.

His face darkened. "I don't believe in coincidence."

"Neither do I," she retorted sharply. "Why were you in *Tenampa* that night? How did you find me in that bar?"

He shrugged. "It wasn't hard. I was following Luis."

"So you've been a part of this from the beginning," she said slowly. "From the very beginning."

"Yes. And I still don't know about you, Lin. Why are you in Veracruz?"

She looked at him for a long moment, at his sea-green eyes, at his sturdy open face, then asked tiredly, "Tell me one thing only, Juan. Are you on Luis' side?"

His face hardened. "No."

"Don't Scream!"

"All right then. I'll tell you everything because . . . . Oh, more than anything, Juan, I want to trust you."

"You can trust me," he said gently.

She sat down on the bed and ran her hand through her hair. "I came to Veracruz because I knew Maura was coming here."

"Are you meeting her?" he asked quickly.

"No, no, nothing like that, but I hoped I could find her and help her."

And quickly, eagerly, she told him of coming in that night after Juan had rescued her from the bar and finding the message from Maura.

". . . and it was pinned to the bed. The note said 'The Irish seeks the true cross.' Well, of course the Irish had to be Maura and the true . . . ."

"Veracruz," Juan interrupted.

"Yes, finally I figured that out. Then Wednesday morning, I searched the Mallorys' apartment . . . ."

"The Mallorys!" he interrupted again. "Why?"

She looked at him in surprise. "Oh I didn't tell you about that. Tuesday morning when I got back from school, I was almost sure that Natalie had searched our room."

And she described the slamming front door and her glimpse of Natalie going up the stone steps to the Mallory apartment and then her trip to the Pawnshop and Tommy's awkward appearance and his attempt to chase the boy and the afternoon that passed so slowly while she and Natalie waited together in the common room.

"And all of it together made me very suspicious of them so Wednesday morning I waited until they'd left and I searched their apartment. They came back and almost caught me but I hid under the bed and I heard them talking about a shipment that they are supposed to pick up off the coast of Veracruz and bring to land."

Juan whacked his hand hard against his leg. "I am a fool!" he exploded softly. "I should have known. Luis is contacting someone at the house of *Señora* Alvarez. I should have known it would be the Mallorys! They are just the kind to be involved."

"But why should you know anything about any of this?" Lin asked unhappily. "You say you aren't in it with Luis. That must mean you are against him. Now if he and the Mallorys are going to smuggle something into Mexico and you're trying to stop it . . . ." She looked at him and her face lightened. "Juan, you must be police of some sort! Are you?"

He smiled. "Of some sort. In your country you have the F.B.I. and the C.I.A. Every country has its counterparts of those famous agencies."

"Good grief!" she exclaimed. "You are a secret agent!"

He shrugged. "Secret agent sounds so dramatic. Let's just say I'm a government agent."

"That sounds pretty dramatic, too," she said happily, "and it also sounds perfectly wonderful. You can't imagine how glad I am to unburden this whole mess on someone who is official! Now you can find Maura and everything will be all right."

"I hope it will," he said soberly. He studied her for a moment. "Lin, I want you to come with me. Will you do that?"

"Of course," she said readily. "But why?"

"I'm going to need your help." He paused, then said, "I got a report on what you did today. You visited the Mallorys' yacht?"

"Yes."

"That's great. I think we just might put one over on the Mallorys, but I need your help to do it."

"I'll do anything I can," she said.

"Thank you, Lin," he said quietly. And then he

"Don't Scream!"

looked down at his watch. "For a start, I want you to come with me."

She pointed at the now closed shutters that overlooked the plaza. "Won't those men see us?"

"Not the way we're leaving. Come on, let's hurry. There's much to do yet tonight."

It took her but a moment to thrust her purchases of the afternoon back into their sack and grab her sweater and she was ready.

Juan led the way up the dim night quiet corridor. They skirted past the stairs to the lobby. At the rear of the floor, Juan pulled open a heavy fire door and pointed up the steps. Lin climbed behind him. On the top floor a short half flight of stairs ended beneath a closed trapdoor. Juan pushed it up and they climbed out onto the roof. In the moonless night they moved, dark shadows slipping through blackness, skirting ventilators and chimneys. He stopped at the parapet separating her hotel from the one next door and helped Lin climb over to the adjoining roof. In no time at all they were padding down the back stairs to the street.

None of the watchers noticed them as they walked down through the sidewalk café and out onto the street. The boy and girl walked quickly, but not too quickly. They turned right on *Figueroa*, which is one block back from the sea and runs parallel to it. They passed small modern row houses with locked front gates giving onto a parking place and then the entrance to the house. It was in the second block that Juan stopped at the fourth house and unlocked the gate. He shut it firmly after Lin stepped within.

"Here we are," he said easily, no longer bothering to lower his voice.

"And where is that?"

"A house I've borrowed from a friend," he said noncommitally. "And the kitchen has even been stocked for guests. Let's get a snack and I'll tell you what I have in mind."

The house, a cheerful yellow without and within, didn't have an air of occupancy. Lin noticed dust along the baseboards and the stale smell of rooms with windows too long shut. But in the kitchen it was cheerful, a pink and white linoleum floor, bright print curtains, a gleaming white wooden table.

And Juan's friend had indeed stocked the small refrigerator and pantry. They lounged at the kitchen table and drank hot chocolate and ate sweet rolls. Lin felt a million miles from trouble.

But when Juan pushed back his cup, she leaned her elbows on the table, ready to listen.

"I want you to tell me everything you can about the Mallorys' boat," he began. "I'm going to hide on board if I can manage it."

A smile slowly spread over Lin's face. She picked up her sack which she had plumped on the floor beside her chair. Wordlessly, she pulled out her purchases of the afternoon, the flashlight, the compass, the black turtle-neck sweater, the black slacks.

"Great minds work alike, of course," he said wryly. "What was your plan?"

She shrugged. "I didn't really have one. I just thought I'd try to get on board and hide and see if I could find out just what the Mallorys were going to do. I thought the more I learned, the better chance I'd have of helping Maura."

"You would do a lot for a friend," he said quietly.

"Yes."

"But you need not go now," he continued. "With your knowledge of the boat, I'm sure I can manage to hide aboard."

She caught his hand. "Juan, don't make me stay behind. I can help, I know I can. And besides, I could be very useful if we were caught on board."

"How so?"

She laughed. "I could tell Tommy and Natalie that you were my date and we had smuggled aboard just for fun. They might not quite believe it, but they wouldn't have any reason to think you were a Mexican agent."

"It will be dangerous. If I am right about all that is involved, it will be very dangerous."

"I can help, Juan."

He pushed back his chair and walked slowly back and forth in the small kitchen, his footsteps solid on the patterned linoleum.

"I don't like it. I don't want to take you with me. I would like to know that you are safe here in this house." He slumped back into his chair and thudded his fist against the table. "But I will do what I do not want to do. I will take you with me because the two of us can perhaps do more than I alone. And so many lives hang in the balance."

He paused and his mouth twisted a little. "So many lives at stake. It sounds like one of the soap operas on daytime TV. But tonight it is true. If the shipment is what I think it is and if it is to be used as I fear, then so many will die."

She clasped his wrist and his quick pulsebeat tingled beneath her fingers. "Are we going to try and stop the shipment?"

"No, it must go through. What matters is where it goes. Then it and the men waiting for it will be stopped."

"If that's what matters, why hide aboard the *Miranda* at all?"

"Because we don't know where she will land." He pushed back his chair and walked to a cupboard above

RENDEZVOUS IN VERACRUZ

the drainboard. He opened the door and the shelves lay bare. He pressed hard against the second shelf and it swung forward, revealing a space behind it. Reaching in, he pulled out a small attaché case.

He set it down on the table in front of Lin.

"Open it."

She undid the catch and lifted up the leather flap.

"It looks sort of like a radio," she said uncertainly.

"It is a sort of radio," he responded. "It's a transmitter. When I flip this button, the transmitter sends out a series of signals on a special frequency. When those signals are picked up, the location of this transmitter can be plotted very accurately."

At her still puzzled look, he continued, "It will pinpoint exactly where the *Miranda* lands her smuggled cargo and men will be able to get there in time to trace that cargo to its destination in Mexico."

"And that is important?"

"That is the most important thing of all. And so, let's get to work." He pulled a pad of paper and a pen from a drawer in the table. "Now," he directed, as he settled in his chair, "tell me everything, everything that you remember about the *Miranda*."

It was very late before they finished. And when Juan showed Lin to a small whitewashed room with a single cot and chest of drawers, she was aching with fatigue. When she closed the door and was alone, she sat for a long time on the cot, too tired even to rest. She stared dully down at her hands and the small Beretta pistol they held. Juan had insisted that she take it.

With a grimace of distaste, she rose and put the gun on the chest of drawers. Flicking off the light, she walked cautiously across the dark room until she reached the cot, then stretched out on it, taking time only to slip out of her shoes. She fell into a heavy but troubled sleep. She woke once toward morning, her breath held tight, then relaxed and sank back into sleep. Atop the chest, the dark blue metal of the Beretta glimmered in the gray light of dawn slanting through the window.

RENDEZVOUS IN VERACRUZ

17
NOT BEATEN YET

Maura turned restlessly on the woven mat. She looked up at the narrow slit that served as the hut's only window. It was now a light patch in the curved bamboo wall and she knew that dawn was coming. Outside it would still be night, really, but the darkness would be melting into a dull shadowy grayness and the first bright spread of sunlight would pulse in the east and swiftly, brilliantly, morning would come to the jungle.

The night, her second in the hut, would be over and *El Jefe* had not come. Maura sat up and brushed her hair out of her eyes. Her fingers still tingled at the unaccustomed stickiness of her dyed hair. Would she ever be glad when she could wash it all out! And then she almost smiled, but not quite. How easily, how confidently the mind assumes the future will come. How unthinkingly she had expected that she would wash the blackness from her hair. And all logic indicated it was questionable indeed.

She stood and walked to the embers glowing on the hearth and added two more sticks of firewood. The sudden blaze of light and warmth swept over her for a moment, then subsided. She shivered.

The girl huddled for a moment over the hearth, her doubly thick *rebozo* tight around her, then abruptly busied herself with making coffee. The unaccustomed task with the awkward tripod occupied her hands, but not her mind.

The night was ending. And she wondered emptily if her decision to not attempt an escape all the day before had been a mistake.

But Ramón had watched her well as Jaime had instructed him. He had showed her a clear pool up a stream that fed into the river and she had washed and filled the hut's clay pot with cool fresh water under Ramón's close attention. All the while she covertly studied the terrain, but the thick jungle growth stretched away on all sides and she knew if she entered it, she might never emerge. Back at the hut, she had looked out on the muddy sluggish river—and she had seen the knobbly back of an alligator. It didn't take much thought to opt for a meeting with *El Jefe*.

But now as the night drained away and Friday dawned, she wondered if she had better faced the jungle or stumbled down the banks of the river, even to be caught easily by Ramón. At least, she would have tried.

The water boiled and she poured the strong hot coffee into a pottery cup. As she drank it, thirstily, hungrily, some of its fire flowed through her and she sat a little straighter. She wasn't beaten yet. She was Maura Kelly and she wasn't beaten yet.

18

ABOARD
THE MIRANDA

Lin should have been sweltering and breathless under the heavy tarp. Its thick weight, permeated with the smell of mildew and oil drippings, pressed against her, but she was too scared to care about either the heat or the odor. She tried to stop the telltale trembling of her hands. She was completely covered by the tarp so Juan couldn't see their giveaway unsteadiness, but she had to get a grip on herself and quickly.

She had plunged into this, insisted upon it. Now she must have the courage to see it through to the end. And, when it was over, she and Juan and Maura would be safe. The danger would be done—if all went well.

The rowboat rocked gently in the swell. The mid-afternoon sun beat down on the tarp, but the warmth couldn't penetrate. Lin's bone-deep chill. Her sense of foreboding ran deep and strong as the sweep of the tide. She shivered and ran through the plan again in her mind. It seemed sure to succeed. What could go wrong?

So many things could go wrong. The thought grew and expanded and filled her mind and she felt colder than ever. With a still shaking hand, she lifted the edge of the tarp just a fraction. It was sharply reassuring to see Juan's legs sturdily braced against the bottom of the row boat. As reassuring as it had been last night at midnight when she sensed another's presence and had been pulled hard against his chest.

Lin risked a soft whsiper. "Anything happening yet?"

"Not yet. I hope Miguel didn't take my *pesos* and decide to go to the movie."

She dropped the edge of the tarp. If Miguel didn't play his role, she and Juan were stymied before they started. She half hoped the boy had gone to the movie, but she knew he would come. He had thought it a lark and been glad to play a joke for his friend whom he had adventurously led aboard the caïque the day before.

And then she heard Juan's soft call of triumph. "Ah, here he comes. Yes, good boy. He's running out on the dock as if it is all so urgent."

Even beneath the tarp, Lin could hear the rattly pound of the boy's bare feet on the wooden boards of the narrow pier.

Miguel's clear high voice carried over the water. *"Señor, señora,* there is a telephone call for you at the Yacht Club. It is *larga distancia*—for the *señor* or perhaps it is the *señora.* I don't know. They told me to run hard."

"Long distance!" Natalie exclaimed. "Who do you suppose is calling us? Nobody knows we are here, except of course, Luis and . . . ."

"Hush," Tommy ordered. "It's probably your mother tracking us down."

"Oh, it is not!" she said irritably. "It's sure to be for you, but I'll come too if you want."

Lin heard them clamber up the narrow gangplank to the pier and the flat slap of their tennis shoes as they hurried over the uneven wooden structure. In only a moment, the door to the Yacht Club opened and closed. They were gone.

She pushed back the tarp as Juan rowed the few yards to the pier. He threw a rope and skillfully made fast. She was right behind him as he climbed onto the pier.

Quickly, half running, they reached the *Miranda,* boarded her and slipped quietly through the open doors of the cockpit housing and down the four wooden steps of the companionway.

"Keep a watch while I take a look around," Juan said softly.

Lin stood midway up the companionway and peered cautiously over the coaming. The dock lay bare and quiet in the thickening heat of midafternoon. Behind her she could hear Juan's swift search of the *Miranda,* the two cabins, the saloon, the galley and the forward storage spaces.

It took him only two minutes.

"Quick. The port cabin. It's the only place to hide."

She followed him into the cabin. The double bunks were unmade. The bottom one held two duffel bags and the top an assorted jumble of extra gear. Juan opened one side of a doubledoored storage space beneath the bottom bunk. An old sail was crammed into it, stiff and yellow with age.

"This is too small for me, Lin, but I think we can burrow a place for you behind the sail. It will be dark and hot, but there should be enough air. See, the cabinets have almost a half inch clearance from the molding. Warped some, probably."

"Where will you hide?" she asked anxiously.

"Up here on the top bunk. I'll pile this stuff even a little higher and squeeze down behind it."

"But Juan, if they search, they'll find you at once!"

"True, but why should they search?"

There was no answer to that.

He smiled briefly. "Don't look so worried, Lin. If they do find me, I don't think they will find you, so I'm going to put my bag of tricks down with you."

"Put what?"

He swung the small attaché case in his hand. "This.

Even if they find both of us, our mission will succeed. It is all set and it's sending continual signals."

In another moment, she and the transmitter were wedged behind the thick folds of the stored sail. And wedged was the word for it. When Juan shut the cabinet door, a wave of claustrophobic panic flooded over her.

Sweat beaded her face. Her breath came in short gasps. She wanted more than anything in the world to tear herself free of that dark cramped space. She held onto the sailcloth and gripped until the tendons in her hands ached. Gradually the panic receded, leaving her limp and half sick.

She had been so self-absorbed that nothing registered but the dark stuffiness of her hiding place. Now as she lay quietly, breathing deeply of the musty stale air, she began to hear the slap of water against the hull, the soughing and creaking of the wooden joints of the *Miranda,* the occasional roar of a motor launch.

A sudden thud jarred the boat. The Mallorys were back!

They passed by the cabins and went into the saloon.

"Well, it really is strange," Natalie said, "but maybe the line was cut off. You know how the telephone service is! If anyone really wants to talk to us, they'll call back."

"Yeah, but it seems funny to me that the operator claimed there wasn't any call at all. Oh well, it was probably a mistake all the way around. Maybe that boy got the wrong name."

"Maybe so."

"I'm hot," he said irritably. "Fix me up something to drink, Nat."

She crossed to the galley and began to chip on a block of ice in the small ice box.

"When are we going to leave?" she asked.

Tommy looked at his watch. "It's about three-thirty now. I thought we'd shove off about five. We can find our spot while it's still light and then kind of hang a-round. That is, we'll leave if somebody brings us some money."

He slumped into a cane chair and moodily thumped the arm rest with his hand.

"And if nobody comes?" she asked.

He slammed his hand once harder against the wicker then sat unmoving. "If they don't show with the money, we have to make the scene out there, but it's not going to be a good deal."

Natalie dropped irregular chunks of ice into a large tumbler, then turned to face him. "If there's trouble, it should be between whoever this Luis fronts for and Mr. Stefanakos. It's not our problem."

"Yeah," the young man responded, but his voice didn't sound convinced. "I have a feeling it isn't going to be so easy."

She brought his drink to him and he downed it quickly, then stood up and took the empty glass back to the galley.

"Want some more?" she asked.

"Later. I need to check the rigging on the jib. D'you know where I put my work gloves?"

"I think I threw them in the other cabin," Natalie replied.

Lin stiffened in her cramped hiding place. Tommy walked into the cabin and crossed to the bunks. She held her breath as he rummaged on the bottom bunk.

"I can't find them, Nat," he complained loudly. "Are they down under here?"

The cabinet door was swinging open. Lin tried to push farther back but the hard wood of the bulkhead held her fast. Tommy was yanking on the sailcloth when the quick patter of Natalie's sneakers sounded in the cabin.

"Oh Tommy, can't you find anything? That's where we stuffed the old mainsail. Your gloves are over here!"

Aboard the Miranda

159

The cabinet door slammed shut and Lin began to breathe again. As Tommy and Natalie left the cabin, amiably bickering, Lin began to tremble with reaction. If much more happened, her nerves would go and she would just quietly crawl out and surrender.

It would be better when the *Miranda* got underway. At least, she hoped it would. Surely the Mallorys would be much too busy sailing the craft to hunt for odds and ends in the cabin they used as a catch-all.

Quietly she pulled her pencil flash out of her pocket and turned it briefly on to look at her watch. Only another hour and a half to go and then it would be much better.

Lin sighed and squirmed a little, trying for a more comfortable position. The Beretta, shoved into the waistband of her slacks, was distinctly uncomfortable. She pulled it free and pushed it beneath the edge of the mainsail. She wished she hadn't accepted it from Juan. She certainly wasn't going to need it. The Mallorys might be involved in smuggling but they weren't hardened criminals. She shoved the pistol even farther away. She hated guns.

19
EL JEFE
COMES

Maura sat as still as a carved relief, her hands twined over one knee. She watched impassively as the patch of sunlight streaming through the door grew smaller and smaller and finally disappeared. Through the door she could see her guard lounging comfortably in the shade of a palm. The sun was far in the west now and the shadows from the palm almost reached the opening into the hut.

It couldn't be long now before *El Jefe* came—if he was going to come. And, somehow, Maura couldn't hope that this strange interlude would end so tamely. He would come.

She sat so quietly that a chameleon darted inside and stopped beside her feet, then darted up and over them in his pursuit of a beetle.

She was aware of the thick afternoon heat and of passing time and of danger, but she didn't think of these things. It wouldn't help.

Instead, she thought of her family and particularly of her tart-tongued but kindly grandmother. She thought of friends and of the way the waves foam and crest and break at Acapulco. She thought of the Roman Forum in the moonlight and the crisp clarity of a winter morning in Taos as she schussed down a slope in immense silence.

It was both a farewell and an affirmation.

She saw Ramón jump to his feet and hurry across the clearing. Slowly, with a fluid grace, she rose and faced the open doorway. A pulse throbbed gently in her throat but she stood calmly, waiting.

Ramón came to the doorway and filled it.

"Come. *El Jefe* wishes to see you."

She walked out into the sunlight and faced the young, strongly built man who stood, hands on hips, wearing combat boots.

They studied each other in silence for a moment.

His hair was sleek and black, his eyes dark and intent, his face narrow and bony. He emanated an air of danger and power and vigor.

His eyes glinted and he smiled suddenly, a quick and reckless smile that momentarily altered his somber, taut face.

"Luis says you are usually a redhead. I can see you would be most attractive."

Startled, she smiled in return, attracted in spite of herself by his lean face and casual grace.

"You don't look at all like a bandit chief," she said.

He laughed aloud. "And you do not look like a thief," he rejoined.

The smile fled her face and she stood even straighter. "A thief?" she repeated evenly.

"A thief."

"I didn't steal the money," she insisted. "I didn't steal it."

"If you didn't, then how did you know there was money in the envelope?" he asked, his voice edged with impatience.

Maura laughed. "I opened the envelope, of course. What woman would not?"

"What did you do with the money?" he demanded.

"I was frightened," she responded quickly. "I looked at all that money and I was absolutely stunned. I put it and the note and Luis' map all back in the envelope and put the whole thing under the clock."

He stared at her. His mouth hardened and he hunched forward and grabbed her arms. "Luis' map! What map?"

She tried to pull away, but his grip tightened. "I don't know what map!" she exclaimed. "It was just a map that Luis scrawled and put in the envelope before he gave it to me. I don't know what map!"

He let loose of her as suddenly as he had grabbed her and she stumbled back a pace.

The bandit chief turned to Ramón and spoke quickly in Spanish, "Get Jaime and Francisco and Luis."

As her guard turned away, Maura saw for the first time the trio standing at the clearing's edge. Luis and Jaime and a man she had not seen before stood where the trail led into the jungle.

Ramón reached them and at his gesture and words the men walked quickly toward the hut. Ramón held Luis by the arm, urging him forward.

The bandit chief half turned. Luis stopped in front of him.

"What's wrong, Carlos?" Luis asked. "Won't she talk? I'll make her talk. Just give me five minutes . . . ."

"She has answered," the bandit chief replied. He spoke almost in a monotone but the tone could not disguise the throb of anger in his voice.

Luis backed away a step. "Is she lying about me?" he asked, his voice high. "I swear I didn't take the money. It all happened just as I told you!"

"But there is something you did not tell me," Carlos Rodriguez said softly.

The muscles in Luis' battered face slackened and Maura knew he was afraid, deathly afraid. The taint of his fear spread over the sunlit clearing and touched Maura with a bone-deep chill.

Luis' eyes flickered to either side where Ramón and Francisco stood. His head jerked and he looked behind him and into the impassive face of Jaime. His head swung back toward the bandit chief.

"What didn't I tell you, Carlos?" he asked and his voice cracked.

"I should have known better than to trust you," Carlos said quietly. "I have dealt with men. Your hands are too soft and your face is too pretty." He paused and looked at the puffy and discolored flesh. "Was too pretty."

The bandit chief stepped closer to Luis. The tough and dangerous man didn't touch Luis but Luis seemed to shrink inside his dirty and crumpled clothing.

Carlos spoke very softly. His voice reminded Maura of the light rustle when a copperhead slithers through dry grass.

"You had two tasks, Luis—you were to pass the money to the Mallorys and tonight, if the shipment reached Jaime safely, you were to hand him the map where my men and I would be waiting."

The bandit chief paused and looked at Luis and his eyes were black and cold and hard.

Maura watched the bandit chief and Luis as impassively as she could since everyone still seemed to assume that she didn't speak enough Spanish to understand what was going on.

The silence now was intense.

Luis tried to speak but couldn't. His cheekbones were starkly prominent now in the puffy mass of his face.

Carlos stepped even closer and Luis flinched.

"The work of two years ruined. The plans made, the men gathered and you drop a map of my camp into a letter just like that!" He snapped his fingers. The tiny sound was magnified in the absolute quiet of the clearing.

Luis swallowed and managed to say, "I didn't see anything wrong with it. I thought Tommy could give the
map to Jaime . . . ."

"And what if *Señor* Mallory was caught off the coast?
You see, Luis, I very carefully planned all of this, the
Mallorys to pick up the shipment and deliver it to Jaime.
And only if the shipment reached Jaime with no trouble,
only then would he have the map to my camp. Not because I don't trust Jaime, but because a man cannot be
forced to reveal what he does not know. And you throw it
into a letter and give it to a woman. If we hadn't caught
her in Veracruz, the American Consul would have that
letter and then the Mexican government would be in-
formed and all my plans would be finished."

"I had taken all precautions so that I wouldn't have
to be on the beach tonight myself. Only Jaime was to
be on the beach with the truck. He was to meet you and
Señor Mallory. From *Señor* Mallory, he would receive
the crates. From you, he would receive the map."

"I will go. Carlos, I will go," and Luis grasped the arm
of the bandit chief.

Carlos shrugged away his touch. He looked at Luis and
smiled and Maura closed her eyes for a moment. It was
a terrifying smile.

"No," the bandit chief said quietly, "You will not go
to the beach. Instead, Ramón shall take you to the camp
—and he shall tell the men what you did."

Luis stared at him and then lunged forward and
grasped the chief by his wrists. "No, no, Carlos. They
will kill me!"

Carlos broke Luis' grip and pushed him back against
Ramón. The bandit chief shrugged and said, "Perhaps
they will, Luis."

Wild and desperate and doomed, Luis swung about
and tried to push past the three men. The one called
Francisco laughed aloud as his fist smashed into Luis'

face. Luis crumpled slowly down onto the ground and lay still.

The bandit chief made no comment as Jaime and Francisco pulled Luis across the clearing and disappeared into the jungle.

Maura looked at Carlos, at the sleek dark head, at the bright compelling eyes. Now she knew that his lean attractive air masked the cunning and ferocity of a wolf.

"Why did you do that?" she asked. "What made you angry with Luis?"

"He made a mistake, *señorita*," El Jefe said in English. "It need not concern you. And now, where is the money and where is the map?"

"I told you," she said quickly. "I put them back in the envelope and put it under the clock."

Quick and violent anger flared in his eyes. "Don't make a mistake with me, *señorita*, as Luis did. I am not a fool. If you didn't take the contents of the envelope, why did you run and why did you dye your hair?"

"Because I knew I had stumbled into something dangerous. I started to go to the Embassy but I saw Luis outside it and then I decided to come to Veracruz. My cousin is an official in the Consulate here. I thought I would come and tell him what I had discovered and he could take the information to the Mexican authorities."

"And what have you discovered, *señorita?*"

She looked surprised and tried to speak in an uncertain tone. "That the Mallorys are smuggling something into Mexico and it's worth a hundred thousand dollars."

"Is that all you know?"

She shrugged. "What else is there?"

"Where are the Mallorys landing their cargo?"

She spread her hands helplessly. "I don't remember the exact latitude and longitude. I just glanced at the message and put it back in the envelope."

"What did the map show?" he asked sharply.

Again she shrugged. "I'm sorry, but all I could think about was the money. The map was just some lines to me."

"And you claim that you put the envelope beneath the clock?"

She nodded.

He grabbed her arms as quickly and viciously as a jaguar seizes its prey.

"Then tell me, *señorita,* how do you explain that *Señor* Mallory called Luis immediately and reported that the envelope was empty, absolutely empty?"

She stood quite still in his grasp.

"I think that's very easily explained," she said steadily.

"Then explain it to me," he said silkily, but the bruising grip on her arms didn't ease.

"*Señor* Mallory reports to you that the money is missing, is that right?"

He nodded.

"Then tell me this, if you don't find the missing hundred thousand dollars, then you must provide *Señor* Mallory with another hundred thousand if you are to get this shipment. Is that correct?"

The bandit chief nodded again.

"How nice for *Señor* Mallory," Maura said softly.

Slowly the hurtful pressure on her arms lessened. His hands fell away and he stared at her.

A half smile curved his full mouth.

"For your sake, *señorita,* I hope you speak the truth."

He turned then to Ramón who waited nearby and directed him to search Maura.

She stood stiffly on the hard beaten earth outside the little hut. The search was quick, efficient and impersonal. Ramón then ducked into the hut and came back with her basket. He pulled out her *rebozo,* which had been neatly folded on top, dropped it to the ground then dumped out the contents of the basket. He tossed aside her passport, gown and watch and poked at the bottom of the basket.

Finally he looked up, *"Nada."*

Maura knelt and gathered up her belóngings.

The bandit chief stared at her for a long moment, then spoke in Spanish to Ramón. "You and Jaime take Luis to the camp."

"What are you going to do?" Ramón asked.

The bandit chief smiled. "The *señorita* and Francisco and I are going to pay a little call on *Señor* Mallory."

They waited until Ramón returned with Francisco. Maura ignored his interested study of her. She rearranged the contents of her basket and wondered if she had been a fool. The bandit chief was a dangerous man but this Francisco, he was more than dangerous. He was deadly.

20
HIS FACE IN
HIS HANDS

The heavy thump on the afterdeck was the first warning. Tommy and Natalie were relaxing in the saloon with
cool bottles of mineral water. Tommy looked up with a
frown and started to rise.

In the port cabin, Lin heard the thump and wondered
who was coming aboard. Juan lay very quietly, the better
to hear, and fingered the Berreta in the waistband of his
trousers.

Tommy was halfway to the companionway when he
stopped abruptly and backed up a pace.

"Who are you?" he demanded.

Then his eyes fell from the face of the intruder tō the
gun in his hand. It was aimed at Tommy's chest.

"What the hell's going on?" Tommy asked angrily and
he stepped to his left to shield Natalie who had risen and
walked up behind him.

"Put the gun away, Francisco."

Francisco lowered the gun, letting it dangle in his hand.
"Sí, Jefe."

Tommy looked past Francisco and saw the bandit chief
with Maura close beside him.

"You must be *El Jefe*," Tommy said, relief quick in
his voice. "But what's the gun stuff for? I'm on your side.

I see you caught Maura. Come on in." Turning he led the way back into the saloon.

He gestured expansively around the saloon. "Come on, sit down. Did you get the money back from her? Jaime said he'd bring it this afternoon."

The bandit chief ignored him.

"The ladies will sit on the settee," he directed. "Francisco, you stand behind them.

Uncertainly, Maura and Natalie moved to the wicker divan and sat down.

Tommy's frown returned. He started to speak, but *El Jefe* gestured abruptly for silence.

"You were expecting Jaime?" he asked.

Tommy, half-angry, half-puzzled, nodded. "Sure. He told us Wednesday morning that the money would be brought to me before we sailed. So, sure I was expecting him. Did you bring the money?"

The bandit chief just looked at Tommy.

The young American waited for a long moment, then said irritably. "What's going on? Did you bring the money or not?"

Again Carlos merely looked at him.

Tommy shrugged finally. "I don't get this at all; but I'll tell you one thing for sure, you won't get your shipment if I don't have the money for Mr. Stefanakos."

"The *señorita* says that she didn't take the money out of the envelope."

El Jefe spoke so softly and unemphatically that Tommy didn't understand for a minute. Then the American's face flushed and he said angrily, "What d'you mean she didn't take it! Of course she did! She ran away. What more proof do you want?"

The bandit chief looked at Tommy and at Maura. Then his gaze fastened on Natalie.

"Your wife is very beautiful, *Señor* Mallory." He

paused, then asked harshly, "Where is the money, *Señor* Mallory?"

Tommy shook his head, "I don't have . . . ."

The bandit chief interrupted, saying, "Francisco."

Francisco had been lounging negligently against the arm of the wicker divan. At the bandit chief's call, he straightened and the perpetual half smile on his face widened just a little.

Francisco was different, very different, from Jaime or Ramón or even *El Jefe,* Maura thought. He was a special kind of man, an especially evil kind of man.

Francisco would be at home in any tough big city in the United States, walking with an arrogant slouch up a ghetto street. Or you could find his counterpart wielding a club behind the protection of a police shield. The kind of man who can be sought in a sleazy Paris bar, a proud veteran of the French secret police.

There is this kind of man everywhere in the world. They naturally gravitate to power in the secret police or as guards in concentration camps or as lieutenants to guerillas.

This was Francisco—his thick black hair slicked close to his head, his long sideburns flared at the end. He was built with the muscular grace of an adagio dancer, but, inevitably, his shoulders slumped a little, his hands hung loose in supreme physical arrogance.

Francisco had the style of the brotherhood, too. He didn't hurry his moment. Insolently, he looked Natalie up and down. Unhurriedly, he clicked the safety on his gun and shoved it into his waistband.

Then, savoring the strained attention of Natalie and Tommy and Maura, he slowly, so slowly, tucked a finger under the cuff of his left sleeve, then, as quickly as the flick of an adder's tongue, he drew out a long, incredibly narrow knife with a handle of ivory and a blade of gleaming steel.

Tommy lunged forward but the bandit chief's fist caught him full in the stomach and he doubled up, gasping for breath.

Francisco pressed the tip of the knife against Natalie's face at the point of her left cheekbone. The skin broke and a spot of blood welled up beneath the knife tip.

The bandit chief hauled Tommy to his feet.

"I will give you one minute. If you don't tell me where the money is, Francisco will move his knife so . . . ." The bandit chief's hand mimed a swift stroke.

Tommy, still swaying from the blow to his stomach, visibly gathered strength to launch himself across the room.

Francisco pressed a little harder with the knife and the spot of blood on Natalie's cheek spread.

Maura jumped to her feet and clutched Francisco's arm, crying, "Stop it. Stop it at once. I have the money. I lied about it. I have it with me and I'll give it to you, but don't hurt Natalie."

"Francisco," the bandit chief said quietly.

Francisco shrugged, wiped the knife blade against his pants, then sheathed it. Implicit in his causal acceptance of the order was the confidence that if not this time, then another his knife would have its victim.

In the port cabin, Juan lowered his Beretta. He wouldn't have to face down Francisco and the bandit chief, after all. He moved away from the door. Intent upon regaining his hiding place as quickly as possible, he swarmed over the end of the bunk and burrowed back down behind the pile of extra gear.

He took a deep breath then and began to relax. It would have ruined everything if it had been necessary to stop Francisco. But he couldn't have lain there and done nothing while Francisco mutilated Natalie.

Juan was very engrossed in his own thoughts.

He must have made some sort of noise as he climbed

up into the top bunk. Small noises of one sort or another usually will pass unheeded aboard a boat. Old woods creak. Water slaps against the hull. But a small noise can signal disaster to those who live with danger. They are alert to a fractional variance from the norm.

The bandit chief didn't move but his whole stance altered. His narrow bony face stilled, his wary eyes slowly circled the room. Peremptorily he gestured Francisco to him, but his voice remained low and quiet when he spoke to Maura.

"Tell me about your lie, *Señorita* Kelly," he commanded, but all the while his eyes shifted and, suddenly, he held a gun in his hand.

Maura spoke uncertainly, not sure quite what was happening. "There isn't much to tell. I just didn't want to give you the money. I saw no reason to make it any easier for you to accomplish your scheme, whatever it is. And I didn't feel I owed the Mallorys anything. But, even so, I couldn't sit there and watch that—that animal hurt Natalie."

Maura looked at the gun, now trained on the open door to the port cabin, and at Francisco. She had called him an animal and she was afraid of him as she would fear a coral snake or a crocodile. He was moving with his sinuous grace toward the port cabin.

Maura's eyes flickered again at the gun and then at the moving man—and the knife in his hand.

She opened her mouth but no sound came. She breathed deeply, then said loudly and sharply and in a voice so high it seemed unrecognizable, "What's he doing? Why is he sneaking into the port cabin with a knife? What's going on around here?"

The bandit chief swept her with a cold and angry glance but he didn't waste time dealing with her. The damage was done. Instead, he moved quickly toward the port cabin and reached it as Francisco slipped inside.

His Face in His Hands

The bandit chief remained in the doorway, covering both the interior of the cabin and the saloon. The gun moved first one way, then the other.

"Don't move. Don't move at all . . . ." And then he called into the cabin, "Look well, Francisco."

Maura's sharp loud questions had warned Juan. He had frozen for an instant only and then he moved quickly, decisively. He shoved his billfold and the gun deep into the space between the mattress and the side of the bunk, rumpled his hair and assumed a bleary expression.

He was slowly lifting his head from behind the junk when Francisco slipped into the cabin. Juan peered about as if his eyes were dim with sleep. His gaze fixed on the knife, his eyes widened and he sat bolt upright, his arms held high.

Francisco stopped and gestured contemptuously for Juan to climb down.

"It's nothing, *Jefe*. Only a wharf rat who had found a soft bed."

"Possibly," Carlos replied, "but be careful."

"Get down," Francisco ordered. "Fast, fast."

Juan did as he was ordered, but clumsily and all the while whining in the slurred thick patois of Veracruz, "I didn't take anything. You don't need a knife for me. I just came on board, running away from a cop, and I though I'd look around, the boat being empty, then the Americans came back and I climbed up in the bunk." He stopped and ran a hand through his rumpled hair. "I fell asleep and I didn't wake up 'til there was a lot of noise. I didn't take a thing."

The bandit chief studied Juan.

"He doesn't look right for a dock thief. Search him, Francisco."

The search unearthed only a few coins, a pocket knife and a crumpled package of *Delicados*.

"Where are your papers?" the bandit chief demanded.

Juan frowned stupidly, then shrugged his stocky shoulders, his hands spread wide. "I didn't take any papers. I didn't bother anything. I just came . . . ."

Carlos interrupted, "Come into the saloon."

Juan shuffled across the cabin and gingerly stepped through the door, walking as far from Francisco's knife as possible. He went into the saloon, his eyes darting here and there.

The bandit chief walked to the middle of the saloon and looked searchingly at Maura and Tommy and Natalie.

"Do any of you know him?"

Tommy slowly shook his head.

Natalie shrugged, "He dosen't look familiar to me."

Maura said blandly, "I 've never seen him before."

The bandit chief stood quietly, his eyes remote, ignoring all of them. And then he shrugged and looked indifferently at Juan.

"It doesn't matter. If you are a thief, you picked the wrong boat to board. If you are a government agent . . . ." Again he shrugged.

He turned to Maura. "You have the money, *señorita,* and the map?"

She nodded.

The bandit's full mouth thinned. "This time your words had better be true. Where are the money and the map? We searched you."

"You didn't search my *rebozo,*" she said tiredly. She pulled the thick black *rebozo* from her shoulders and flung it at his feet. "The money is sewn inside, along with the map. It's really two *rebozos* sewn together."

The bandit chief nodded at Francisco, who quickly picked up the shawl and slit open one side. He thrust his hand within and pulled out the thick packet of bills and the cream colored envelope. He handed all of it to Carlos.

Carlos counted the bills, then opened the envelope and pulled out the rendezvous message and the scrawled map.

His Face in His Hands   175

The last he tore into tiny pieces. Crossing to an open port hole, he thrust out his fist and the shreds whirled away and down into the water.

He paced back to the wicker divan where Tommy sat with his arm around Natalie. Tommy's face was flushed and his blue eyes sullen.

The bandit chief looked down at him. "Does your stomach hurt, *Señor* Mallory?"

"Go to hell," Tommy replied violently.

"You don't seem to have profited from your lesson, *señor*. You don't seem eager to cooperate. Am I to understand that you refuse to make the pickup of the shipment?"

"You can understand exactly that!" Tommy said. "I won't touch any of this with a ten-foot pole. You and your funny friend can just go out and pick it up yourselves."

"No."

El Jefe spoke softly but the atmosphere in the saloon chilled and hardened.

"You can't make me do it," Tommy said loudly. "There are people all around, passing up and down the boulevard. Before you can fight all of us, we'll make so much noise and rumpus that everybody will come running. And you, Mr. Carlos whatever-your-name-is, you'll be caught right in the middle of it."

So quickly the eye could scarcely follow the movement, *El Jefe* pulled free the knife sheathed at his belt and pressed the blade against Natalie's face.

Then the bandit chief smiled. "I hope you learn your lesson this time, *señor*. I well understand that you can create a great disturbance. But, long before anyone reaches this boat, it will be forever too late for your wife."

Tommy sagged back in the divan. "We'll pick up the crates," he said dully. "We'll pick them up."

"Yes," *El Jefe* agreed. "You will do exactly that." He shoved the knife back into its sheath then gestured to Francisco. "Quickly now, tie up *Señorita* Kelly and the stowaway."

In only a few minutes, Juan and Maura, arms and feet tightly bound, were dragged into the starboard cabin and dumped on the floor. Francisco hooked the door to the cabin wall so that they were in full view from the passageway.

Carlos nodded. "All is ready. You can get underway now, *Señor* Mallory. Here is the money."

Tommy took the bills and stuffed them into his shirt pocket, his face grim.

El Jefe crossed to the table and looked down at the chart of the bay. His finger traced an inked line. "This is your course?"

"That's it," Tommy said gruffly.

"The rendezvous is outside the twelve-mile limit. It will take you about two hours under power, right?"

Tommy nodded.

The bandit chief studied the chart carefully, then said abruptly, "Make me a copy of this."

"But why on earth . . . ?"

"Do as I command," Carlos said sharply.

Tommy shrugged and quickly traced the course on another map.

Carlos compared his copy with the original, then tucked it inside his shirt. He swung around and moved to the couch.

"Francisco, you are to cast off as soon as I leave. When you are well underway, out of sight of land and unobserved, you are to throw the excess weight overboard." And he spread his hand toward the starboard cabin and the trussed forms of Juan and Maura.

For a moment there was only a stunned silence and then Tommy and Natalie spoke at once.

His Face in His Hands

"You can't!" she cried. "That's murder!"

"I won't do that!" Tommy shouted. "You've gone too far."

Carlos ignored them. Pulling Natalie to her feet, he began to move toward the companionway, shoving her ahead of him.

Tommy surged across the room but Francisco blocked the way, his knife a shining deadly menace.

El Jefe looked back over his shoulder.

"You understand, *Señor* Mallory, your wife will be returned to you if you follow your orders."

At the foot of the companionway, the bandit chief paused and motioned Francisco near.

Tommy tensed as if to jump, but Francisco's eyes never wavered and the knife waited.

Carlos whispered briefly. Francisco nodded, then the bandit chief and Natalie turned and climbed the companionway and were gone.

Tommy stumbled to a chair and sank into it as if life and will had drained from him. He stared for a long moment at the empty companionway and then buried his face in his hands.

21
MAN
OVERBOARD

Lin could feel the slap of the waves against the hull and hear the throb of the diesel as the *Miranda* moved slowly out of the harbor. She pressed down the stiff folds of the sailcloth and eased open the locker door.

She lay there, listening and tasting the bitter flatness of fear at the back of her throat. She swallowed but it didn't help. And every minute, every second, the *Miranda* plowed farther from the shore, out toward the open sea. And, when it was an empty sea, when there were no boats nearby, then . . . .

Lin yanked the Beretta from beneath the hard lump of sailcloth. She held the pistol tightly in her hand. For a moment longer, she shrank in the compartment, her face resting on the sailcloth, its canvas rough against her cheek. Then slowly, carefully, she pushed the locker door wide open.

She listened again and now she listened for her life and Maura's and Juan's.

The *Miranda* rose and fell as she drove through the water. The old wood creaked and strained. Waves slapped against the hull. The diesel throbbed.

But no one moved below deck.

As quietly as a fish gliding through water, Lin crawled over the sailcloth and out onto the floor of the cabin. She closed the locker door, then stood up. Still listening, she clicked the safety off the Beretta, then stepped close to the bulkhead and eased along it until she was next to the open doorway.

Was Francisco below deck or was he up top, helping a grim-faced Tommy to maneuver the Miranda? Everything depended upon the answer.

Lin stood there, pressed against the bulkhead and stared around the cabin. She knew that however long she was graced to remember anything, she would remember that cabin, the durable and luxurious teak bunks, the handpegged floors, the careless mounds of the duffel bags and extra gear piled on the unmade mattresses.

Sunlight slanted through the open porthole. The *Miranda* was moving steadily through the water. How long would it be before Francisco attended to his little chore?

Where was Francisco?

Lin knelt and as slowly as a mudbank oozes, she moved her face even with the door.

She saw him the instant her face cleared the doorframe.

Francisco swaggered even when standing still. He lounged at the far side of the saloon, looking out the starboard porthole of the doghouse.

She gradually pulled her head back, then closed her eyes for a moment, but the picture didn't go away. Francisco looking out the porthole, looking to see if the ocean was empty, looking to see if it was time to drag Juan and Maura up the companionway and thrust them over the railing and watch them plummet down into the water.

Wearily she pulled herself upright. She stared down at the gun in her hand and a tide of revulsion swept through her. She hated guns. A gun has but one function and that is to destroy. And guns destroy as human beings those who shoot them just as surely as they destroy those who are shot.

She steadied her hand and eased close to the doorframe,

then very quietly stepped out into the doorway. She raised her hand and pointed the gun at Francisco. For a long moment, she trained the gun on his back and then her hand wavered and fell slowly to her side. She fled back into the cabin and leaned against the bulkhead, this time for support.

She couldn't do it, no matter what the cost or what the provocation. It didn't matter that he planned to kill. It didn't matter that even with the gun she would be no match against his knife if he came after her. And if it cost her life itself, it still didn't matter. She could not shoot another human being in the back.

She looked dully down at the floor, knowing within herself that Francisco wouldn't hesitate to slaughter a roomful of unwarned people. But she wasn't Francisco.

And then the girl tensed. Francisco was walking across the saloon, his steps soft but purposeful. Had he heard her? Was he coming to the cabin?

Her lips trembled but she brought the gun up until it pointed toward the door. If he came into the cabin . . . . And then the catlike steps were past. He was going up the companionway.

He was going above deck. Of course, she thought coldly. He had to be sure the way was clear before he undertook his grisly task.

She didn't hesitate at all. Perhaps he would be right back down, but she couldn't wait to find out. There was so little time left for Maura and Juan.

Lin hurried across the passageway and into the starboard cabin.

Maura and Juan lay on their sides. As her sneakers scuffed softly on the floor, their heads turned toward the door. And, in that first instant, their faces reflected their fear, the skin tight drawn, the eyes so determinedly blank.

And then they realized it was Lin and the masks of fear broke and their faces reformed and came to life.

"Don't just stand there," Juan said huskily. "Come right on in. It's good to see you."

"And why don't you close the door behind you," Maura urged. " I do so hate drafts."

The fear which had driven Lin for so many hours fled and she smiled. Turning, she unhooked the door, closed it and shot home the bolt. And then she hurried to Juan. She would feel a lot safer when he was mobile again. She knelt, lay her gun on the floor and began to tug at the ropes around his wrist.

The knob on the door rattled viciously.

Lin flashed one terrified glance at the door, then bent once again to the knots. "A knife," she cried. "I need a knife or something sharp. I can't get these knots loose."

"Natalie's hand lotion!" Maura called.

Lin hesitated and looked blankly at her roommate. "What?"

"Break it. Quick. Then use the pieces to cut with."

Lin swarmed to her feet and hurried to the dressing table and grabbed the bottle. As she held it above her head then crashed it down hard against the rim of the lower bunk, the doorknob rattled once more. Almost immediately it was still and footsteps pounded toward the companionway.

The bottle shattered against the bunk and soft white hand cream oozed over Lin's fingers and onto the floor. She whirled around and knelt again by Juan.

Francisco's footsteps thudded overhead.

Tommy shouted, "What's the gun for?"

Lin frantically wiped her hands against her slacks and tried again to get a grip on the thickest piece of the bottle, the cap and neck and a long irregular shard of glass. Her greasy hand slipped until she clamped hard onto the piece and felt the sharp edges cut into her palm.

A shot boomed through the open porthole and the bullet thudded into the bulkhead behind Lin. Francisco was hanging over the side of the Miranda and shooting through the porthole!

The girl bent closer to the ropes and thrust the sharp shard of glass in between the cords and sawed back and forth. Blood ran down her fingers from the cut on her palm but she pressed harder and harder and as the second shot thundered into the cabin the ropes fell free.

Juan grabbed Lin's gun and rolled over on his stomach to fire up through the porthole.

As Juan's shot sounded the diesel engine abruptly fell silent and the *Miranda* hove to and began to rock. Juan fired again at the porthole as Lin sawed desperately at the bonds around his ankles.

A shot rang out above deck but it wasn't aimed into the cabin. Tommy swore loudly and stumbled on the cabin housing above their heads.

Lin plunged the shard of glass up and down, up and down and abruptly the ropes fell apart. On his feet as quickly as a cat Juan reached the cabin door, unbolted and opened it and was gone.

Overhead there was a sudden thud of rushing feet, a strangled gasp and then a heavy splash. Lin scrambled to her feet and headed for the door.

Maura's voice stopped her. "If I have to go, dear one, I'd rather do it on my own two feet. Hurry and cut me free."

Lin swung around and hurried to Maura. She sawed through the ropes then helped Maura to her feet. As they moved toward the door, they heard Juan shout, "Hold it! Wait a minute!"

The girls ran out of the cabin and hurried up the companionway, but at the top Lin put a cautionary hand on Maura's arm and they poked their heads carefully over the coaming.

Standing on the roof of the doghouse, Tommy steadied himself against the lashed down boom. In his left hand, he held outthrust a grappling hook. Blood seeped across his right shirt front. And flecks of blood stained the curving claws of the hook.

Juan balanced on the edge of the deck, a few feet beyond Tommy's reach.

"Put it down, Tommy. I'm not threatening you," and Juan shoved Lin's gun into the waistband of his slacks.

Tommy swayed but he didn't lower the grappling hook.

"I won't turn back. I have to get that shipment or Natalie . . . ." His words trailed off, but he stood a little straighter. "I'll fight until we're both gone, but I won't go back."

"I know that," Juan said gently. "I don't want you to turn back. I want to pick up that shipment just as badly as you do."

Tommy stood stolidly on the planking, unsteady but determined.

"You don't understand," the American said grimly. "I mean I'm going to get those crates and deliver them to Carlos whoever-he-is."

His shirt front was sopping now and blood trickled steadily down his arm to drop from his hand and splatter redly on the cabin housing. He hunched forward a little and raised his left arm even higher, the grappling hook glinting in the sunlight.

Juan nodded and spoke very slowly. "That is exactly what I want to do, Tommy. Get the crates and take them to *El Jefe*."

Slowly, slowly Tommy lowered the grappling hook. He looked steadily at Juan.

"I'll kill you if it's a trick," he said simply.

"No trick," Juan replied as simply.

Tommy nodded. As the necessity to fight faded so did his strength. The grappling hook dropped from his hand, clattering to the deck, and Tommy sagged against the boom.

Juan hurried to him and helped him slide down onto the planking.

Maura and Lin clambered over the coaming and knelt by Tommy, too.

"Quick, Lin," Juan said. "Get a sheet. Let's staunch this flow, then we'll see to the wound."

Lin whirled around and hurried below.

Maura grasped Juan's wrist. "What happened? Where's Francisco?"

"Overboard."

"Shouldn't we look for him?" Maura asked. "He'll drown if. . . ."

She trailed off as Juan shook his head. The Mexican pointed down at the grappling hook, "Francisco tangled with that."

She looked at the thick metal rod and the curved claws, speckled with blood, and her face whitened.

Juan finished unbuttoning Tommy's shirt as Lin clattered back with strips of clean white cloth and a pan of water. Juan pressed a swath of cloth against Tommy's wounded shoulder.

"How did it happen?" Maura asked quietly.

Juan continued working on the wound as he explained, "Tommy couldn't take it when Francisco started potting shots through the porthole. He knew it wouldn't take much to wipe us out. He cut the engine, grabbed the grappling hook and went after an armed killer. Francisco winged him, of course, but that's the last thing he ever did. Tommy saved us."

"And lost Natalie," Tommy mumbled in a flat and empty voice.

Juan gripped his uninjured arm. "Don't be a fool. We won't let you down. We'll get Natalie back or die trying. I promise you that!"

Tommy lifted his head and a faint light of hope glowed

in his eyes. "You think we can do it? But what about Francisco? Won't *El Jefe* . . . ?"

Juan shook his head. *"El Jefe* doesn't care about Francisco or any other thug who follows him. He wants those crates. And to get them he is going to hand over Natalie safe and sound."

Tommy struggled to get up. "Let's go get those crates. Let's go!"

Maura gently pushed him back down. "If you get up now, pal, you'll start the blood to flowing again and you'll end up so weak you couldn't down a teddy bear in a pillow fight. Relax. We'll fix you up, then we'll get underway."

22
CRATES OF DEATH

It was a furtive and hurried rendezvous. In the thick black of the moonless night, the tramp steamer crept close to the *Miranda*. A light flashed twice, then twice again. Tommy flicked a flashlight covered with red cellophane in answer. Once, twice, a third time, he snapped the red light on.

The steamer cautiously moved closer, a huge dark shadow in the night.

Tommy and Lin waited tensely on the deck of the *Miranda*. Hidden below in the port cabin were Maura and Juan.

Lin stood beside Tommy, waiting. She answered generally to the description of Natalie so there shouldn't be any question made. But her throat seemed strangely dry as the freighter came nearer and nearer.

When it rode only a few yards from the *Miranda's* bow, a searchlight suddenly stabbed through the darkness to pinpoint Tommy and Lin on the deck of the caïque. It flashed off in only an instant.

"Mallory?" a harsh voice called.

"Mr. Stefanakos?" Tommy responded quickly.

"Yes. Do you have the money?"

"Yes."

"We will heave a line. Make it tight, then come aboard."

The lights of two flashlights wavered then settled on the deck of the *Miranda*. The Greek contraband runner was taking no chances. The flashlights wouldn't be nearly as visible as the bright swath of the spotlight.

Lin shared the Greek's anxiety although for a very different reason. Natalie would be lost if the shipment didn't reach *El Jefe*.

The line snaked through the air. Tommy caught it, knelt and made it fast to the starboard cleat.

And then he called to Mr. Stefanakos, "Please, can one of your men come aboard for the money? I injured my shoulder in a fall yesterday and I don't think I can make it."

No answer came for a long moment and then, once again, the stabbingly bright light of the searchlight sprang to life and it raked the *Miranda* end to end before stopping on Tommy.

The American shaded his eyes with his left arm and hunched forward.

The Greek called across the water. "If this is a trap, you are a dead man."

Tommy put his hand gingerly on his right shoulder. "It's no trap."

There was a low-voiced exchange. The spotlight went out and, with agile swiftness, a seaman from the freighter swung hand over hand down the line and landed with a thump on the deck of the *Miranda*.

Tommy pulled the packet of bills from his shirt pocket and handed it to the man who turned without a word and began his ascent back to the ship.

The satisfied call came quickly then. "Good enough, Mallory. Good enough. I'll send down your ten thousand dollars and two of my men will come aboard to make the transfer of the crates."

More quickly than seemed possible two sailors swung down the rope and landed on the *Miranda*. The first, dark, thickset and muscular, handed Tommy ten bills.

The American held them in his hand for a long moment. Lin held her breath, then relaxed as he jammed them in his pocket without comment and swung around to go aft to the engine.

The diesel rumbled to life and Tommy hurried to the wheel. The *Miranda* edged even closer to the freighter. Finally, the Greek called, "Hold her steady, now."

Lin moved back closer to the mast and away from the forward deck where the two seamen waited in readiness.

Suddenly a small motor purred to life on the deck of the freighter, wood grated against metal, and out of the blackness into the dim light of the two wavering flashlights appeared a crate.

Slowly the crate swung out, suspended from a boom, until it hung above the deck of the *Miranda*.

It wasn't going to be a marshmallow roast to make the transfer, Lin realized. When the boom was over the deck, then the tackle attached to the mast of the derrick would lower the crate. But it would only work if the *Miranda* held steady. The *Miranda* rolled in the troughs of the waves even though she was lying to leeward of the freighter. It was no mean feat on Tommy's part to maintain the *Miranda* the right distance from the freighter— too close and the side of the *Miranda* would buckle against the steel plates of the freighter, too far and the crate would dangle over the ocean.

It took more than an hour to transfer five good-sized crates, each about four feet long and three feet deep, and three smaller boxes, each roughly the size of a shoeshine boy's kit. Each crate was carried below after the freighter crewmen disengaged it from the tackle ropes.

When the last crate thudded to the deck of the *Mi-*

randa, Lin blew a sigh of relief. It was almost over, almost done. She stretched and realized then how stiffly and tensely she had stood that long hour, waiting for discovery, waiting for the arrival of some curious ship that could bring disaster to all of them.

She was almost lighthearted as the crewmen swung up the rope, back to their ship. And when the freighter eased off into the night, she hurried to the wheelhouse.

"Come on, Tommy, let's go. Now we can go get Natalie."

"Yeah," he said gruffly. "In a minute."

He turned the *Miranda* head on to the seas, then hurried aft and cut the diesel. Lin followed him, asking, "What's wrong? Can't we go?"

Ignoring her, Tommy turned down the companionway and, once below, walked straight to a locker in the saloon.

Maura and Juan looked up in surprise. When Tommy turned away from the locker, a crowbar in hand, Juan moved toward him.

"Wait a minute, Tommy. What do you think you're going to do?"

Tommy looked up and seemed to see them for the first time. His jaw tight, his cheeks sunken in with fatigue and pain, his eyes cold and remote, his face was ages older than when Lin had first seen him.

He spoke harshly. "I don't think anything. I know what I'm going to do."

He reached the first crate and jammed the wedge-shaped end of the crowbar beneath the lid and began to push down.

Juan moved, his hand outthrust, but Tommy was faster. He pulled the bar free and raised it high in the air.

The Mexican shook his head. "That's not necessary," he said quietly. "I told you, Tommy, our goal is the same. We both want those boxes delivered and your stake is higher than mine. So why do you want to louse it up?"

Tommy lowered the crowbar a little.

"You hit the ball on one thing, Juan. My stake in this is higher than anybody's. And from this point on, I don't take anybody's word for anything. I'm going to find out what's in those crates so I'll know why they're so important to *El Jefe*. The more I know, the better I can fight for Nat."

Juan nodded. "So your idea is to check out the crates, then close them up again. Is that right?"

"That's my idea and that's what I'm going to do."

"All right," Juan agreed briskly. "Give me the crowbar. I'll open them up for you."

Tommy looked at him stonily and made no move.

"Believe it or not," Juan said impatiently, "we're on the same side. I don't plan to break your head in two. I thought I would jimmy them open so you wouldn't start bleeding again. But suit yourself."

The American flushed. "Sorry." He handed the crowbar to Juan and stood by, watching.

The contents of the big crates came as no surprise to the little group bunched around Juan.

"All assembled and everything," Tommy said slowly.

"The better to kill people with," Maura commented coolly, but her voice shook a little.

Juan held up a semi-automatic rifle. "An M-1. Sterling condition. Worth a fortune to the right buyer."

"Isn't that an American Army gun?" Lin asked, puzzled. "How did they ever get a load of those?"

Juan shrugged. "Not all shipments reach their destinations in time of war."

"War?" Maura repeated, "But I thought we used M-16's in Viet Nam—the rifle there was so much fuss about."

The Mexican nodded. "The latest American rifle is the

M-16 and it was used in Viet Nam. It's lighter than this one," and he weighed the M1 in his hand. "But the price is better on the black market for the old M-1's and M-14's. They aren't so likely to jam."

"If the U.S. uses M-16's now, then where did the M-1's come from?" Lin asked.

"Korea, probably," Tommy said listlessly. "There's always graft, particularly in Asia. Somebody greased a palm and got who knows how many guns, and they've been selling them ever since and making enough money to enjoy the air in Monte Carlo and Biarritz."

Lin frowned. "From Korea? But that was years ago! I mean, are these guns that old?"

Both Tommy and Juan smiled, and the Mexican said dryly, "Guns aren't like bananas. As long as they don't get wet, they'll keep forever."

Tommy ran his fingers over another one of the rifles. "Mr. Stefanakos said we would be bringing in antiquities," he said dully. "We wouldn't have done it, if we'd known it was guns."

"Ten thousand dollars as your cut and you thought it was antiques?" Juan said skeptically.

"Ten thousand dollars," Tommy repeated emptily. "It sounded so simple." He looked up at Lin, a plea in his eyes. "It sounded so simple. All we had to do was pick up these crates and deliver them a little way up the coast and we'd have ten thousand dollars."

He pulled the bills out of his pocket and his mouth twisted. "I got the ten thousand all right—but I don't have Natalie."

The American thrust the money at Juan. "Take it. It can be part of your evidence when this is all finished."

And he began to nail shut the opened crate.

"I'm a little slow, my friends," Maura said quietly, "but the pieces are beginning to fall into place and I think the picture's cockeyed."

Lin looked at her in surprise. "What are you talking about?"

"Doesn't anything about this nightmare strike you as a little strange?" Maura asked.

No one spoke, but understanding glinted in Juan's eyes.

Maura looked at him. "You know the answer," she said swiftly. "It's obvious that you are a Mexican agent and it's pretty darned obvious that no wild and woolly bandit chief needs this kind of arsenal," and she flung her arm wide to include all the crates. "I mean, what does he intend to rob? The national treasury?"

Juan nodded sombrely. "You are very quick, *señorita,* and you are right. Carlos Rodriguez is not just a bandit chief. He has been a bandit chief to suit his own purposes, to store up enough cash to make this purchase and that is why he is so determined that he shall have this shipment. You stirred up a pretty nest of rattlers when you took the envelope with the money."

Lin looked at the crates with new eyes. "But what on earth does he want all those guns for?"

It was Maura who replied. "I think he must fancy himself another Fidel."

"Fidel Castro?" Tommy asked. "But Mexico isn't anything like Cuba."

Juan's face hardened. "No, Mexico isn't Cuba, but it could happen here. Castro started out with a handful of men in the mountains and he began with a promise of a new life to the people."

"And you think Carlos Rodriguez could do the same here," Maura said.

"There is unrest here in Mexico." He looked at the three Americans in turn. "As there is unrest in your country. The students take over Columbia University in your country. Here they have rioted in the *Zócolo* and been killed in the Plaza of Three Cultures. There are many who see much to be done in Mexico and they will follow a man on horseback. But that isn't the way. Mexico has done so much, traveled so far on the right road. It has taken time. It will take more time—but we can do it and do it without armies marching across the land and people dying. So many will die if Carlos gets these guns."

"Then why are you so hot to deliver these crates to him?" Lin demanded.

"A plant doesn't die if you lop off the flower. We must dig out the roots. It will do no good to simply stop this shipment. Carlos will rob more banks and arrange for another shipment. What we must do is trace the shipment to its destination, to his camp, and capture him and all of his men. It is men who make revolutions, not guns," Juan said.

It was very quiet in the saloon as Juan opened the rest of the crates, then shut them one by one. Three more big crates held M-1's. The fifth big box was filled with grenades and the three smaller crates were ammo boxes, holding hundreds and hundreds of bullets.

"So there you have it," the Mexican said tiredly. "A man who sees violence as the path to change—and he doesn't care who gets hurt along the way."

Tommy pushed away from the bulkhead. "You don't have to tell me that. I've learned it." He paused and rubbed savagely at his face. When he spoke, his voice was indistinct, distorted with emotion. "Juan, do you really think Natalie will be all right?"

"I think she is safe at least until we rendezvous to deliver the crates."

"But then . . . ."

"We will demand that she be returned to you before we unload the crates," the Mexican said.

"What if he refuses?" Tommy asked.

"We will do all that we can," Juan promised.

"All that we can," Tommy repeated slowly. Tears

burned in his eyes. He rubbed his hand roughly over his face and quickly walked to the table and bent over his chart.

Juan joined him. "Where are we supposed to land the crates?"

Tommy pointed to a cove a little north of Veracruz. "That's the spot." He frowned. "If I angled north a little, we would get there sooner, but I don't guess it matters. The rendezvous is set for midnight and, besides, when Francisco came above the last thing that he told me before he went down to drag you all up was to be sure and stay absolutely on course, both in going out and coming back in."

Tommy gave a sudden harsh exclamation of pain as Juan gripped his right arm.

"What did you say?" the Mexican demanded.

Tommy, his face pale, pulled Juan's hand loose. Half-angry, half-puzzled, he demanded, "What's all the excitement? It was when Francisco came up, just before he found the door to the cabin locked. He told me to be very sure that I followed the course marked on the chart both going out to meet the freighter and on the way to the cove."

"Did *El Jefe* take a copy of the chart with him?" Juan asked tensely.

Tommy nodded.

"I should have known," Juan swore. "I should have known!"

"Known what?" Tommy demanded, his voice laced with worry.

"I should have known *El Jefe* would take no chances." He looked at Tommy, his eyes grim. "Don't you see? Too much has gone wrong. He won't take a chance on the cove now or on you and Natalie."

"What do you mean?" Tommy asked.

"Before Maura intercepted the message and the map,

he didn't have anything to worry about. You and Natalie would land the shipment, then sail off, happy with
your money from Mr. Stefanakos and sure to keep quiet
about it because you were smugglers. But that's all
changed now. How can he be sure that Maura didn't
show the message or the map to some one before she was
captured? He can't risk that possibility."

"So you think he'll meet us at sea?" Tommy asked.

"Yes. And I don't imagine he intends for you and
Natalie to be free to sail off and warn the Coast Guard."

"But if we cooperate to that point, why wouldn't he
let us go."

"You know too much. You know who he is. You know
what he plans. Alive, you could perhaps reach the Coast
Guard in time to alert everybody to him and his boat."

Juan looked around the saloon. "Dead, you can't tell
the Coast Guard anything." He glanced down at his
watch. "We have time enough," he muttered. "Just
barely time enough. Listen hard because our lives depend
upon it . . . ."

23
RENDEZVOUS IN VERACRUZ

"Ever played softball?" Maura's voice carried clearly over the wash of the water as the *Miranda* plowed through deepening troughs. A freshening wind from the northwest was raising flecks of white on the waves.

Lin swallowed, trying to ignore the uncertain feeling in her stomach as the bow rose and fell. To her, it seemed to sweep up and down in an alarming fashion. She managed a ragged whisper in return.

"A long time ago."

Lin closed her eyes and for an instant she could smell the hot dust and dried grass of an August afternoon and feel the sweaty hide of a softball in her hand. She tightened her grip on the small ridged grenade, so like a miniature pineapple.

"I never could throw worth a darn," she added. She loosened her hold a little on the grenade and thought unhappily that her long ago softball certainly hadn't prepped her to lob grenades at anybody. In fact, nothing had prepared her for that!

She and Maura were sodden dark lumps pressed against the deck on opposite sides of the bow in the shadow of the railings. They were wet and they were going to be wetter. Every time the *Miranda* dipped her nose down and then struggled up against a wave, water cascaded over the bow, then sloshed out the scuppers, drenching them thoroughly in the process.

The water was cold and salty and sticky. And then the rain began, light at first, a thin dripping rain. But, as the wind picked up, the rain came harder, little needles of cold spitting down onto the deck.

Lin fingered her little pile of grenades. She had four of them, cupped between her body and the railing. She went over it once again. Juan had explained it very simply. Pull the pin and throw.

With her left hand, Lin held tight to a cleat on the deck as the pitch of the *Miranda* increased. She was very cold now. The wind gusted, the water rolled over them and pelted down on them. But her hands felt moist and hot.

Pull the pin and throw. How could she possibly even pull the blasted pin out with her hands as slick as cellophane? And what if she managed to pull the pin out, then dropped the grenade? What if it slipped out of her hand and rolled loose on the deck of the *Miranda* with the bow pitching and the rain falling and the water sloshing aboard. . . . Oh good grief, what if she dropped it? To drive away the horrid visions in her mind, she called out huskily, "Did you every play softball, Maura?"

"Yes," came the gay reply. "And I had one grand moment of glory. I pitched a no-hitter. I was in the fifth grade and it was the game of the year, girls versus the boys. I will admit to one moment of temptation. I had a crush on Willy Kruger and when I had him at two strikes and three balls, I almost gave him a hit for love's sake."

Lin laughed a little. "What happened?"

"My homeroom teacher was the girl's coach and I guess she knew her kids. She stood up from the bench and called, 'Maura Kelly, keep your mind on your work!' I stood there for a minute, then I fanned that plate like

RENDEZVOUS IN VERACRUZ

a jet breaking the sound barrier. First, last and always, I'm a pragmatist."

Lin laughed in earnest. "So now, pragmatical to the end, you're going to give your all for the home team and lob those grenades like mad. Right?"

Maura hissed, "If you don't mind, darling, let's not assume it's to the end!" She paused, then added, "I'm also an incurable optimist."

Lin made no response. It would take, she thought, more than rampant optimism to see them through this night. But Maura's unfailing cheer had helped. She no longer felt quite so close to panic. After all, there was no valid reason why she couldn't throw something no bigger than a fat orange.

The *Miranda* heaved on through the water, her bow meeting the waves head-on. The deck swooped down then lunged up, down and up. Lin pressed her face against the wet wood and concentrated on the dull prod of a nail-head against her cheek. Time shredded into an indistinguishable gray mist. There had never been a past and would never be a future. There was only this interminable present with the rain pelting down and the water surging over the prow and the boat plunging down and up, down and up.

"Lin. Lin!"

The urgent whisper penetrated the thick muzziness that enveloped Lin. She took a deep breath and lifted her face.

"Lin, we're slowing down. Something must be happening."

Lin's heart began to thud and suddenly her queasy stomach was gone. Reaching out, she pulled close to her chest the little pile of grenades. She breathed shallowly and quickly, straining to hear through the night.

The *Miranda* was certainly slowing down. Tommy

had turned her so that she no longer took the force of the waves on the bow.

Suddenly a shaft of light cut through the rain-riven night to sweep the *Miranda* fore and aft before fastening upon the wheelhouse. Lin pushed even closer to the railing although she was well hidden in the shadow of the overhang.

So Juan had been right. *El Jefe* wasn't about to chance a transfer on shore. And Juan must be right, too, in thinking *El Jefe* didn't intend for any of them to survive this night.

Of course, at this point, the bandit chief would believe that Maura and Juan had already been thrown overboard. He would think the *Miranda* held only Francisco and Tommy. And they must all pray that on this rain-drenched night he would see the two men garbed in heavy sou'westers and accept them as Tommy and Francisco.

She wondered miserably if Juan's plan to outwit *El Jefe* had any chance of success at all.

Behind her she heard Tommy shout, "Drop that beam. I can't see a thing."

Lin raised her head and twisted enough to look aft. Tommy had stepped outside the wheelhouse and stood facing the other craft, his left arm shading his face against the hard glare of the searchlight.

There was no response for a moment, then the light dropped until it pointed into the sea. Very carefully, Lin pushed up until she could peer over the railing.

She chanced only a quick look. As she dropped back to the deck, she felt her first spark of hope. The old lumbering boat that rode so low in the rough water was just a fishing vessel. Why, they would have a chance to run from an old boat like that! Now, if they could just get Natalie safely aboard!

With the light still pointing down to the sea and the

Miranda shrouded in darkness, Lin risked another look over the edge of the railing.

"What's happening?" Maura whispered. The girl lay tight against her side of the *Miranda,* not daring to move into a crouch because only the shadow of the railing protected her from the view of the other craft. Lin, on the other hand, was well hidden by the starboard railing.

Lin continued to look for a moment, then ducked down and whispered, "It's an old fishing boat. And I can see Natalie in the wheelhouse with *El Jefe.*"

The two boats were bow to bow and stern to stern now, separated by about fifteen yards of swirling foam-flecked water.

El Jefe shouted over the water. "Do you see your wife, Mallory? She is safe and will soon be with you—if you cooperate."

"I'll cooperate. But how do you expect to transfer the crates in this kind of sea?"

"The cargo will be transferred," *El Jefe* called. "Stand by to receive a breeches buoy."

A seaman moved to the edge of the fishing boat's deck, a heavy line in his hands. He waited until his boat and the *Miranda* were even, then flung the rope across the water.

A weighted end clanked onto the deck near the wheelhouse. Juan, moving awkwardly in the heavy raincoat, scrambled to grasp it before the rope slithered over the side. He grabbed it, then clutched the railing to avoid pitching overboard as the *Miranda* rolled in a trough.

Struggling back to balance, Juan pushed away from the railing and moved toward the mast, pulling the line with him.

Tommy lunged out of the wheelhouse and grabbed the line. Juan hesitated, then turned away and hurried into the wheelhouse to take over the wheel.

Dismay surged through Lin as Tommy began to haul himself up on the lashed boom. He shouldn't try to climb that swaying boom with his injured shoulder! He should have let Juan do it. But the girl could understand and admire what drove him up and onto the boom. Tommy knew that not only the crates would hang above that roiling sea. The line must hold for Natalie.

In the rain with the *Miranda* rolling first to port then to starboard as the waves surged against her broadside, Tommy seemed to crouch forever on the boom, his hands moving slowly and carefully.

"He's splicing it," Maura whispered.

Lin nodded and risked another quick glance over the side. In the harsh light from the fishing boat, the water flecked and foamed. The boats were about ten yards apart now, a very close and dangerous distance.

If the line failed, if Tommy didn't secure it well enough, Natalie wouldn't have a chance. If she plunged into that turbulent water, she would be whirled toward the *Miranda* and the driving screws of her propeller.

Tommy worked slowly and carefully.

El Jefe shouted once, demanding speed. Tommy didn't even turn his head. With his left hand, he made a very final chopping motion. *El Jefe* didn't call again.

Strangely, in the midst of the storm, it seemed very quiet aboard the *Miranda.* The mast creaked. The waves hissed. The rain slatted against the deck. But a stillness enveloped the two bobbing boats with Tommy the center of a concentrated quiet.

When he finished, he pulled hard on the line. Then, with his good arm, he swung onto the line and held for a long moment before dropping heavily to the deck.

How near collapse Tommy must be Lin thought unhappily. And this was just the beginning.

El Jefe, leaning against the railing of the fishing boat, yelled to the bogus Francisco that the breeches buoy, altered for straps to be buckled around the crates, would be pulled back and forth by whip lines.

Tommy walked slowly and purposefully across the slanting deck and leaned against the *Miranda*'s railing and motioned *El Jefe* to silence.

"Natalie first," Tommy yelled. "Not a crate leaves this boat until Natalie is aboard."

24
THE FINAL CHOICE

The rain swirled down. The wind gusted the waves to a frothy milkiness in the light of the down-turned searchlight.

El Jefe, a dark and stolid shadow at the railing of the fishing boat, stood immovable, his head hunched forward.

Lin could imagine his thoughts. After all, why not return Natalie first? He wanted her back on board the *Miranda.* Natalie was to die on the *Miranda.* And, of course, the bandit chief thought Francisco was the second figure in the yellow oilskins. What could go wrong with Francisco on the caïque? Why not Natalie first?

It took him only a moment to decide, but it was an age that they waited aboard the *Miranda.*

"Of course, *Señor* Mallory," the bandit called. "By all means, your wife first. But do remember that I must have my crates in return. Your wife is to remain above deck. Several of my men are excellent shots, let me assure you."

He turned and gave quick orders to the seamen standing by the mast where the breeches buoy dangled from the thick hawser stretched between the boats. It was a common type of breeches buoy, shaped like a life preserver with a canvas seat attached. To it had been added thick canvas straps to fasten to the crates.

One man nodded and, when the fishing vessel rode

higher in the water than the *Miranda,* gave the buoy a hard shove. The pulley at the top rolled smoothly down the hawser. The seatlike contraption swung wildly above the sea, but it reached the *Miranda.*

Swiftly, eagerly, Tommy fitted up a whip line for his use, then the bandit's crewman pulled the buoy back across the water with his whip line.

Now the buoy was in business. Tommy and the seaman could use their whip lines to steady the load and maneuver the breeches buoy back and forth between the boats.

On the fishing boat, Natalie climbed awkwardly into the ring and sat, her legs dangling, in the canvas seat. The seaman held the buoy tight until the fishing boat rode high in the water then shoved and the buoy began to slip down the hawser. It came fast, faster, and Tommy cried, "Hold the line taut. Slow it down."

The buoy was running down the line too fast, much too fast. The seaman on the fishing boat yanked his whip line. The buoy swung wildly over the water, tipping far to the left. At the sudden increase in weight, the seat holding Natalie split and she began to slip. She clutched hard onto the sides of the ring.

A crosswave as high as a garage door rolled between the boats and engulfed her and the buoy.

Lin peered over the edge of the railing. She wiped the rain from her eyes and stared through the night. It was an agonizingly long time that the water loomed, its foamy crest high, obscuring the buoy. And when the water fell away, Lin began to breathe again. She hadn't dared to hope, but Natalie still clung to the wet buoy.

"Hold on, Nat. Hold on. Hold on." And Tommy's cry was a command and a prayer and a plea.

He began to pull on the whip line, slowly and carefully, though Lin knew he must want to heave the buoy across the water for fear another huge wave might come.

When the buoy was yet a few feet from the *Miranda,*

Tommy leaned far over the rail and grabbed Natalie around the waist. When the buoy swung over the deck, he helped her to the deck.

Drenched and trembling, she turned into his arms and pushed her face down against his neck. He held her as if he would never let go.

"Quickly now," *El Jefe* called. "I have kept my bargain. You keep yours."

Tommy ignored him and bent over Natalie, talking quickly. After a moment, she nodded and moved away from him to the wheelhouse. As she took over the wheel, Juan joined Tommy on the deck.

And then they set to work. One by one, they lugged the heavy crates topside, slipping and swearing as the *Miranda* rolled from starboard to port from port to starboard in the heavy seas. It was hard to keep their balance as they carried a crate up the companionway and onto the rainswept deck. It was hard to buckle the canvas slings around the precariously balanced crates. It was backbreaking and exhausting work but one by one the crates swayed across the water to the fishing boat. *El Jefe's* men worked hard too, lashing the crates to the shifting foredeck of the fishing boat.

Juan and Tommy were wrestling the last crate into place, Juan bearing the brunt of the weight while Tommy pulled the canvas straps around it.

It wouldn't be long now Lin realized. When that crate reached the fishing boat *El Jefe* would make his move. The bandit chief would believe that Francisco held command. They would have a moment of surprise. And perhaps just perhaps they might succeed because the old fishing boat certainly didn't look as though she could run them a race.

The crate was midway between the boats now. And although *El Jefe* didn't know it, the Mexican authorities were already plotting the location of the contraband.

RENDEZVOUS IN VERACRUZ

Juan's small attaché case was now aboard the fishing boat, snugly packed among the M-1's in one of the big crates. Even now it was sending out its measured signals and a man, earphones to his head, was plotting its beeps. All the way to shore the transmitter would signal the course of the boat. If all went well, the unloading of the crates would be observed by unseen eyes and the guns would be traced to their destination and the would-be guerrillas, and their arms would be captured.

All of that, Lin felt sure would happen. But of the fate of the *Miranda* and of Juan and Tommy and Natalie and Maura and herself, she felt no certainty.

The crate wobbled over the railing of the fishing boat and men grabbed it eagerly and loosened it from its straps. The transfer was complete.

Lin crouched on her hands and knees and pulled her little pile of grenades close. She tried to swallow, but she couldn't. She risked a glance toward the *Miranda's* wheelhouse. Natalie gripped the wheel and Lin knew that she was ready, that Tommy had told her of the plan in their low-voiced exchange when she came aboard.

"All the crates are secured," *El Jefe* called across the water. "Stand by, Francisco, to come aboard on the buoy."

Juan waved a hand in answer, but *El Jefe* couldn't see his left hand which was hidden behind the railing. It held a long sharp knife.

Everything happened at once.

When the buoy was midway between the boats Tommy picked up a rifle which had been hidden inside the wheelhouse, shouldered it and shot out the big searchlight.

The *Miranda's* diesel roared to life and the boat lurched as Natalie swung hard to port.

Juan sliced through the thick hawser to free the *Miranda* from the fishing boat and Maura and Lin rolled to their knees in the bow.

Maura pulled the pin and lobbed her first grenade just

past the bow of the fishing boat, just as Juan had instructed. Their plan was not to sink the boat but to create a diversion to escape.

Lin felt a surge of despair. Her hands seemed an uncoordinated mass of thumbs. As she struggled to pull the pin on her first grenade, Maura coolly threw a second and then a third grenade.

Lin tried again and her grenade bobbled out of her hands.

"Get down," Maura yelled.

Lin was down, all right, hunting for that lost grenade. She found it, pushed herself up, threw it overboard in the general direction the fishing boat, then was smacked flat on her back as Maura's grenades went off, one, two, three.

She felt as if a giant hand had flung her hard against the deck. The quick booming explosions were followed in an instant by her tardy grenade.

El Jefe's men, surprised into shocked immobility at the splintering of the searchlight and the surge of the *Miranda,* responded quickly and violently to the explosions of the grenades. The rattle of a machine gun sputtered viciously and bullets thudded into the cabin housing of the *Miranda.*

Lin felt tears hot and hurtful in her eyes. Machine gun bullets spattered across the deck—and they had lobbed their grenades well free of the fishing boat.

Her every muscle aching and sore, Lin forced herself to her knees and she flung out her hands, trying to find her other grenades.

The machine gun fell silent as the *Miranda* pulled farther away into the safety of the darkness and storm. The boat lunged and pitched as Natalie gave it all the power the little diesel had.

Lin had found two of her grenades and was still hunting for the third when she saw Maura struggle to rise, fall back, then slowly, hurtfully pull herself to her knees.

Quickly Lin turned toward her, but the girl called fiercely, "Go ahead with your grenades. I'll be all right."

Maura took her own last grenade, pulled the pin and threw it, but it went only a little way into the darkness before plopping into the water and Maura sank back to the deck.

Lin hesitated, but Maura called again. "Go on. I'm all right."

Lin found her third grenade and peered through the night. About 20 yards away she could see the dark hulk of the fishing boat. A sudden upsurge of water, the result of Maura's grenade, struck the side of the *Miranda*. Lin managed to stay on her feet. She started to pull the pin from one grenade, then stopped. Maybe it wouldn't be necessary. The fishing boat wasn't in pursuit at all. She rode in the water, her engine only idling.

And then a sharp crack sounded across the water and a high whine screamed through the night. A shell rocketed over the *Miranda* and crashed into the sea, perhaps thirty yards ahead.

And Lin knew coldly and without doubt that they and the *Miranda* were doomed.

The shell from the mobile rocket launcher exploded underwater. Water geysered high into the air. A huge fast wave thrown up by the exploding shell traveled swiftly across the water and slammed into the *Miranda*. Water surged up and over the railings. The boat staggered, rolled hard to starboard, then slowly righted and the water sluiced off.

When the wave struck, Lin and Maura were flung hard against the starboard railing and water swirled over them. Lin felt as if a thousand icy hands plucked at her, pulling and tearing, but she clung to the railing.

As the *Miranda* righted, Lin checked and made sure

Maura was still there and then she pulled herself back to her feet and looked across the swirling water at the fishing boat.

She clung to the railing with one hand. In the other she held the one grenade left her. All the others were gone, washed overboard.

The fishing boat held its fire for the moment, but Lin wasn't deceived. The wave thrown forward by the explosion had dissipated but now a heavy swell was surging toward the *Miranda* and, beyond her, the fishing boat. When it passed, their end was sealed. The rocket launcher would fire and, if need be, fire again. But they would find the *Miranda*'s range and the *Miranda* would be kindled and all aboard her would be dead.

Lin took her time. The fishing boat was about 30 yards away now. She pulled the pin, waited for a moment, then drew back her arm and threw with all her strength toward the foredeck of the fishing boat. And then she dropped to her knees and pushed down Maura, who was struggling to rise.

She held her friend and waited and suddenly a dull boom sounded and almost immediately the violent thundering explosion of the ammo boxes splintered the night. Flames flared high into the sky then swept with the force and fury of a furnace the length of the fishing boat. And then, as the fuel ignited, a final heavy shuddering boom signaled the end of the fishing boat and of *El Jefe* and his men.

25
"THE MEN ARE THERE NOW . . ."

Natalie gently pulled the tourniquet a little tighter around Maura's leg and the welling flow of blood on her thigh began to subside.

"Do you think that's too tight?" Natalie asked Lin anxiously.

Lin pushed her draggled hair back out of her eyes. "Well, let's keep it like this for a minute, then we can loosen it."

Maura managed to murmur, "Yes, do loosen it if my foot turns purple. I think that's a bad sign."

The two girls made Maura as comfortable as possible on the wicker divan in the saloon. They wrapped her warmly in two heavy wool blankets and finally sat back on their heels to look at her.

"How do you feel?" Lin asked softly.

Maura's eyes, huge and dark in a whitened face, still contained a glint of humor. "Lots better than if that machine gun bullet had hit me on the first go-round and not as a ricochet," she said dryly.

"There is that," Natalie agreed with a grin. "In fact, I think we can all find a few bright sides if we think about it for a minute. If it weren't for Lin, you wouldn't even be needing a bandage right now."

Natalie got up and went to a locker and pulled out a

battered pigskin case. She returned to the divan and upended the contents on her lap and looked at them ruefully. "Tommy always did tell me that my first aid kit wouldn't cut it if the Bengal raiders struck and I'm afraid he was right. Look, I think these are a painkiller." She opened up a small green box that held four rather dusty off-white pills.

Maura looked at them without enthusiasm then shrugged. "As long as you gay gunrunners don't dabble in LSD, I'll chance it. After all, it's a long, long way from here to wherever we're going to go."

Natalie brought a cup of water from the galley and Maura downed two of the pills. And then the girls were quiet, Maura resting on the divan, white and still, and Natalie and Lin on the floor nearby.

They waited without speaking. The *Miranda* surged twenty yards one way, then turned heavily and beat the way back through the same waters, quartering the rainswept tumbling sea for any survivors of *El Jefe's* boat.

The silence lengthened and grew heavy. Natalie finally burst to her feet. "I think I'll make some coffee," she said tensely.

Lin hunched on the floor and listened and stared dully at the passage to the companionway. How could anyone have survived that tremendous blast? And if, by some miracle, anyone had survived the explosion, how long could they have lasted in that surging, heaving water?

She leaned her head against her knees. How many had been aboard that boat? She couldn't know. Dear heaven, she didn't want to know. Because it was she, Linda Prescott, who had blown them all into oblivion. She wanted desperately to cry, but no tears would come. She wanted to jump up and run, but here was no place to flee.

Her shoulders slumped a moment later. The *Miranda* had picked up speed. She was leaving. The search was over and it had been fruitless.

She heard the weary clump of Juan's shoes as he came down the companionway but she didn't lift her head.

The *Miranda* was pitching hard now as Tommy drove her through the waves head-on. Juan stood at the bottom of the companionway and slipped out of his oilskins. He tossed them on the floor out of the way, then looked wearily around the saloon. His glance fixed on Lin's bent head. Swaying with fatigue and the motion of the *Miranda,* he crossed to her.

"I smell coffee. Come on, Lin, let's have a cup," he said gently.

Lin didn't answer. She only shook her head and pressed it harder against her knees.

He waited a moment, then knelt beside her. "If you hadn't thrown that grenade, we would all be dead. You had to choose. Don't ruin it."

"Ruin it?" And she lifted a drawn face to look at him.

"Yes, ruin it. It took courage to throw that grenade. It takes courage to accept the consequences of any choice. You have destroyed, yes. But that isn't the only truth. You have saved, too. You have saved Natalie and Tommy and Maura and me. You must look at all the consequences. If you had not chosen to throw the grenade, you would have destroyed us. So you must have courage and look at all the truth and not shrink from the fact of killing or from the fact of saving."

She looked at him for a long moment and the torment in her eyes began to lessen. Slowly she reached out her hand and he took it.

"All right, Juan," she said finally. "I will look at all of it."

He smiled then and pulled her to her feet and held her close. "That's my girl," he said huskily. "And now, let's have some coffee."

Together, his arm around her shoulders, they crossed to the galley.

"The Men Are There Now . . ." 213

"Me, too," Maura called after them. "That pill's made me feel like the gritty gray insides of a mattress. I think some coffee would be great." She hesitated, then asked quietly, "You and Tommy didn't find anything, Juan?"

"Nothing," he said. "Nothing and nobody. Bits and pieces of wood, an oil slick, but the rest is gone."

Natalie braced against the drainboard of the galley to pour coffee into four mugs. "Why so somber? I think its good riddance. Why should you care? They were going to tear Mexico apart. Now you don't have to worry about them or their guns."

Juan took a deep draught of the coffee, then said tiredly, "No, we won't have to worry about those guns. But, you see, there are always more guns. In this world, there are so many guns. We didn't want to stop the guns. We wanted to stop the men who would shoot them. The men who want to burn and destroy and kill. The men who want to drench my country with blood."

"But *El Jefe* was killed!" Maura objected.

Juan shrugged. "He was the leader and he is dead, but his men remain in a hidden camp, waiting for him. And there is always another leader waiting, a man who has thought he should have been the leader anyway. I don't think *El Jefe*'s men will melt away. I think someone else will weld them together and lead them."

He looked at Natalie and Maura and Lin.

"You think it can't happen?" he asked. "You think this is only a small band of outlaws, leaderless now, and so it doesn't matter? I tell you a disciplined group of guerrillas will find another leader. The only hope is to capture them all, break the group apart until there is no one to lead or be led."

He dumped two heaping teaspoonfuls of sugar into his coffee, but when he drank his mouth twisted as if the taste were bitter.

He stood there, his face angry and anguished. "So you see why I care that we can't trace that shipment and trap those men who would destroy us!" He looked across the saloon at Maura. "This afternoon when you gave that map to *El Jefe,* you held in your hand the paper that could have saved so many lives." He hesitated, then asked with painful intensity, "Did you ever study the map over? Do you think you could remember what it showed? You see, the men are there now, waiting for *El Jefe* to return with the guns. If we only knew where the camp was . . . ."

Maura's lips curved in a small but exceedingly satisfied smile. "My old Spanish grandmother advised me long ago that the squirrel survives the winter because he keeps the nuts that he garners."

Slowly, with evident effort and pain, she struggled to sit up and push back the heavy blankets. Lin crossed to the divan and pulled the blankets away.

Maura looked down at her long rumpled dress. "My grandmother also favors modest clothing for young women, but even she would think this dress a bit too much."

"It must be the medicine," Lin said worriedly. "She's delirious."

Juan's shoulders slumped. "Yes, it's all caught up with her. It was too much to hope that she would remember the map."

Maura ignored them. "Natalie, some scissors, please. I just don't like this dress."

"Of course, Maura," Natalie said soothingly. "Don't let that dress worry you." She rummaged in a drawer in the galley and pulled out a pair of scissors and hurried to give them to Maura.

She grasped the scissors, lifted her hem and began to cut, talking all the while, "Yes, I'm sure it will look lots better once I get rid of some of the hem. Hmm, here's something!"

All at once very serious, she peeled back the cloth and carefully eased out a damp sheet of paper.

She spread it open and held it out toward Juan.

"Here's your map. I made a copy of it and the landing instructions—and I hope you catch every last one of them!"

26

"NOT AGAIN, MAURA!"

In the golden haze of early afternoon, seagulls skimmed over the water in search of food, an occasional pleasure boat sailed by and children built castles in the sand while their mothers gossiped and watched them. It was quiet and lovely and peaceful in the shade of the palm trees, but Lin couldn't relax in her deck chair.

"Look at that sky!" Maura exclaimed as she swept her hand toward the horizon. "It's the most innocent baby blue I've ever seen! And last night, sheets and buckets and torrents of rain!"

Lin reached out for her glass of lime punch. "I don't complain about last night, pal. I didn't think then that we'd ever live long enough to enjoy another day like this one. Besides, we should be grateful it was just a passing storm and not what the *Veracruzanos* so blithely call a *norte*. The chambermaid told me with very expressive gestures just what happens when a *norte* strikes Veracruz. It stays and stays and the ocean just rolls and rolls. And this is the time of year for *nortes*. If it had been one last night, none of us would have made it home again even without *El Jefe* trying to bomb us."

"Believe me, darling, I'm not complaining." Maura stretched, then muffled an ouch.

"Hurt a lot?" Lin asked sympathetically.

"Nope," Maura said. "In fact, I'm embarrassed that I tumbled down on the deck like a collapsible chair. The doctor was so casual. 'Just a flesh wound.' He said I came unglued because of shock. I thought I was tougher than that."

"Good grief!" Lin cried. "A little flesh wound! I thought it looked awful."

Maura grinned. "I did too, to tell the truth. But I guess to a doctor used to patching up sailors after a hot shore leave, it must have looked pretty minor."

Maura stretched again, a little more carefully this time, and sighed happily. Lin looked at her and wished she could be as relaxed but she couldn't until she knew Juan was safe. Had they caught the men? Had there been a gun-fight when they surrounded that camp in the cold and wet hours before dawn?

The girl looked down at her watch for at least the thirty-fifth time since that morning. It seemed years ago and not just early that morning that a Veracruz policeman had brought her and Maura to the hotel a few miles down the coast and registered them under false names.

"To keep you from having any unfriendly visitors until we wrap this up," Juan had said when they left the boat in the harbor and he turned Maura and Lin over to their protector who even now was lounging nearby on the beach.

And now it was afternoon, a beautiful balmy afternoon, but Juan hadn't come.

Lin sat up straight and said miserably, "Oh Maura, I do wish Juan would come. What if something went wrong when they tried to capture *El Jefe's* camp?"

Maura reached across to pat her arm. "Don't worry, honey. Your Juan is a very capable fella. He'll come."

"I hope so," Lin said very quietly.

"I wonder what'll happen to the Mallorys," Maura said quickly.

"I hope they don't get in too much trouble," Lin said. "If it weren't for Tommy, Francisco would have gunned us all down in that cabin. What did the man at the Consulate say when you talked to him on the phone this morning?"

Maura shrugged. "He moaned a lot. The State Department does so hate for Americans to get mixed up in this sort of thing."

Lin rubbed her cheek. "Do you think the Mallorys are in jail?"

"Well, smuggling guns into Mexico isn't calculated to win you any buddies down here."

"Oh, I know it. And they should never have gotten mixed up in anything like this at all, but they didn't think it was guns. They wouldn't have done it, if they'd known."

"True, but that probably won't cut much ice. Look, give me a hand and I'll hobble in and ring up the Consulate again."

They were midway across the beach when Juan ran down the stone steps from the promenade, his face alight with pleasure. He looked fit and happy and excited, not at all as if he'd been going hard for thirty hours straight without sleep.

Lin deserted Maura and ran to him.

"Everything's all right, isn't it?" she cried.

He lifted her up and whirled her around before setting her down with a kiss on each cheek.

"Linda *mía*, this is a great day. We got them all without a shot being fired, Luis included. And he's singing a very helpful song." He turned to Maura as she hobbled up. "And we owe it all to a couple of *Norteamericanas*," he said gaily.

"And to the Mallorys, too," Lin said quickly.

Juan's face sobered. "Yes, we do owe them a lot and I'm relieved that my superiors see it that way, too. Tommy and Natalie have listened to a pretty stiff lecture, but they got some thanks, too. They'll be out here in a while to join us for dinner. I've planned a celebration for all of us."

It was a very gay group that evening. The food was delicious, the wine tart and the conversation exhilarating.

Lin bent near Juan, listening with close attention as he sought to explain the finer points of deep sea fishing. He was deep in a description of his struggle with a crafty tarpon when Lin felt a gentle touch on her wrist.

She half turned toward Maura.

With the black rinse washed out of her hair and the deep red sheen set off by a filmy green cocktail dress, Maura had drawn glances of admiration all evening. Now she leaned close to Lin to whisper, "Darling, get a load of him!" And she nodded toward a lean and dark Mexican with a craggy interesting face.

As Maura spoke, her glance and the Mexican's met. He smiled and bent his head. Maura smiled in return.

"Oh no!" Lin cried. "Not again, Maura! Not a dashing stranger! How could you?"

The redhead flashed a delighted grin. "Darling, how couldn't I?"